Circle of Love

TRACY BROOKS

iUniverse

CIRCLE OF LOVE

iUniverse books may be ordered through booksellers or by contacting:

iUniverse
1663 Liberty Drive
Bloomington, IN 47403
www.iuniverse.com
1-800-Authors (1-800-288-4677)

ISBN: 978-1-5320-6491-3 (sc)
ISBN: 978-1-5320-6492-0 (e)

Library of Congress Control Number: 2019901305

Print information available on the last page.

iUniverse rev. date: 02/19/2019

ACKNOWLEDGEMENTS

To my mother, Luretta Ware; sister, Rhonda "Kay" Brooks; niece, Nekia Williams Carter; BFF, LaTonya Hutchison; Cousin, Roslyn Sherrill; My prayer partner, Veronica Billingsley. Very special sister-friends: Michelle Sherrill-Austin and Linda Hobbs Kelley.

I took a peek in the dictionary and found these ladies' names listed under the words FRIEND and ENCOURAGER: DyAnn Brooks, Patricia Bell, Jacque Malone, Evelyn Perkins, Eleanor Harris, Sandra Davis, Sharon Burrell, Connie Hall, Jeanette Taylor, Stella Butler, Alicia Griffin and Toni McHenry.

Special shout out to Natalie K. Owens for that extra NUDGE…well actually it was a strong PUSH!

To all of you lovely ladies listed, I extend my sincere thanks for your support and unwavering love.

To my Pastors, Rafer and Natalie Owens,
Faith Inspirational Missionary Baptist Church, Compton, CA
I admire the examples you are.

Pastor Robert A. Williams, Jr.,
McCoy Memorial Baptist Church, Los Angeles, CA
I love you more.

To my Lord and Savior Jesus Christ, THANK YOU!
You make all things possible and You do all things well.
Times of doubt you continuously remind me, *"YES YOU CAN!"*

Romans 12: 3
For I say, through the grace given unto me, to every man that is among you, not to think of himself more highly than he ought to think.

Romans 12:18
If it is possible, as far as it depends on you, live in peace with everyone.

Friends
Are
The
Family We Choose

Family
Isn't Always In
The
Bloodline

CHAPTER
One

I sashayed around my bedroom grabbing clothes to throw on after letting my mother out. A quick peek outside made it crystal clear that I wouldn't be in the house long, it was absolutely beautiful outside, and as one of my girlfriends always says, "I'm gettin' up outta here today."

And, that's exactly what I planned to do as soon as I got dressed. I didn't feel like putting on makeup either, sometimes you don't feel like all that. I'd just cover my little imperfections with sunglasses and hit the road, that was good enough for me.

There wasn't a time when my mother was in my presence when I didn't pause and thank God that at 80-plus years of age this ball of fire was of able body and mind and getting around just fine.

As she always says, "Oh I'm still kicking, just not as high."

I watched as she made her way to her car. As usual, she played that I love you, I love you more game. I laughed as she got the last one in as she pulled away from the curb in her black Cadi, hollering out the window, "I love you more!!!!!"

Still laughing, I made my way back inside the house, but not before taking in the strong smell of the Gardenias on the porch, and hearing the birds chirping. I don't think I'd ever heard them chirp so loud, for a second my mind wondered how birds communicated.

I felt the need to pause for a moment as I leaned against the door closing it. I was overwhelmed with gratefulness, realizing that many of my friends in my age group were now in that role reversal situation where they were now taking care of their parents. Their time was no longer their own.

I recently heard someone say, which describes it well; they were now the one changing the diapers of the person who once changed theirs. So true. I've heard some of the older generation say it a bit differently, but it still amounts to the same thing, *once an adult, and twice a child*.

I smiled up towards heaven and whispered a word of thanks to the Lord above that Moms was still able to get around on her own. *Thank you Lord.*

I headed towards the kitchen for my Fitbit...*and my Apple watch*, putting them both on, one on each wrist; I wondered how many crazy people were as obsessed as I was, wearing two exercise tracking devices. When friends asked why I wore both I always justified it in some whiny voice, "Well, they both do different things."

My girlfriend, Tonya, jokingly called me a nitwit for wanting a Fitbit; she made a little song out of the rhyming words: nitwit and Fitbit. She thought it was utterly ridiculous that someone needed to count their steps, not understanding the fun competition of it all. "Girl that's just another useless electronic device, just get out there and walk for an hour, who needs to count steps?" But, guess who has a Fitbit now? Yep.

Mom made more frequent visits lately, and quite often I asked myself why in the world did I buy her an iPad, after all who else was going to help her learn it, but me. Truly I didn't know if she was going to go crazy trying to learn it, or if I was going to totally nut up trying to teach her how to use it. It often called for way more patience than I could muster up, but, at least she was trying, and at least I knew her brain was still working, or at least trying to, even though we questioned it sometimes.

"I know y'all don't believe it sometimes, but I'm clothed in my right mind. I've got more sense than some of y'all who are way younger than me. Shoot wasn't it just yesterday when Brooklyn was running around looking for her glasses? That girl turned the house upside down, only to find them on top of her head. How's that for good sense? When I walked inside of her house the girl was frantic."

"What's wrong?"

"I'm trying to get out of here for my doctor's appointment, but I can't find my glasses."

"Have you looked on top of your head?"

Mom absolutely loved telling stories like that. She'd laugh so hard she'd have to get a Kleenex to dab the tears of laughter that flowed down her face. Another story she loves to tell is the time Lawana from church took her to the doctor. Lawana needed to make a phone call, but when she went to grab her phone out of her purse she had actually brought the cordless phone from her house with her, instead of her cell phone.

I dared not tell my mother that I too had taken my cordless phone to work one day. She wouldn't have ever let me live that one down.

I can hear her now, "And y'all want to question who has good sense around here, I've got all my marbles."

It was conversations like this that made me ever so grateful that the role reversal situation hadn't come my way. She was funny, spry, and healthy. Thank you Lord.

Before Mom arrived this morning I woke up feeling as though the Lord had scooped out an extra dose of "feel good" my way. I don't care what anyone says, some days are better than others, and today I felt as though I was sitting on the mountain top.

I sang along to the gospel music playing as I got dressed. *I looked in the mirror, what did I see? Another one of God's miracles looking back at me.*

I felt so good I found myself singing both the solo and background parts of the song. Ol' girl was gettin' down, if I must say so myself.

Unlike other people I was encouraging through some things lately, I felt at this time in my life the sun was shining…and mighty bright I might add. I felt good. Oh it's not that I don't have things I'm dealing with. My bills come every three weeks like everyone else, but I have nothing pressing on me. Also, I'd like to think after weathering a few storms in my life that each one that comes my way now doesn't buckle the knees like the first storm did. I've finally learned to be like the water on a duck's back, and let some things just roll right off. I've come to a point where a lot of things don't bother me anymore, and I've also realized every battle isn't mine to fight. But more than anything else, I've learned to take things to the altar and leave them there.

I woke up feeling free! I felt light, as though nothing was weighing me down. My mind was clear. I didn't feel as though my shoulders were sloped from life's pressure. Hey, my bills were paid. I had food on the table. I had clothes on my back. I looked down and even saw that I had shoes on my feet. Oh, and a few extra pennies in my purse. I'm good, and anything else I'll deal with later.

I grabbed a jacket, my cell phone, and keys and continued singing, adding a little dance to it. I had a bounce in my step. *He is a miracle worker.*

The thought of leaving my cell phone at home crossed my mind; honestly it crossed my mind many days. I'm just keeping it real, some days you don't want to be reached. You want to exhale from it all. But, that 5'3" ball of fire I call Mom, was the reason I'd never leave home without my phone.

In my normal way of doing things, (which some have said is OCD), I checked the stove to make sure it was off, I turned again and checked it even a second time. I've often questioned myself as to why I do that every single day. It was especially funny today because the stove hadn't been on in three days. Like clockwork, I check it each night, even though I know I didn't cook a thing, and I check it at least three times each morning before leaving the house. I silently chuckled at myself as I did one more double check of the doors making sure the house was secured, as though something had changed since the last time I checked them…a few minutes ago. I hit the remote; the lady came over the intercom telling me that the alarm was set, and to exit.

I was still singing as I opened the door, but I froze in place as I was startled by my cousin, Shay, stepping onto the porch. I was instantly perturbed at myself. *If you didn't have to check the stove and recheck the stove and recheck the doors, and go back and recheck the stove, you would have totally missed her.* Ugh. I'm not big on people dropping by, but I guess sometimes that rule doesn't always apply to family…at least that's what Shay felt. I silently chastised myself through gritted teeth, *why didn't you check the security cameras as you always do before stepping out, then you would have seen Shay pulling up and avoided her?*

Cousin Shay is the cousin I call my "small dose" cousin, meaning I can only take her in small doses. A full dose of Shay can wear anyone down. It wasn't always like that, growing up she was my favorite cousin. Quite honestly being that neither of us had sisters, our parents felt we were more like sisters than cousins, and truly that was the case *back then.*

Just as any other female cousins would do, we played with dolls, combed each other's hair, polished nails and had tea parties. If we argued they were minimal and we were back in one another's faces within ten minutes. If I can recall our only real disagreement when we were younger was when my mother bought us both Crissy dolls. Crissy dolls were Black female dolls. I named mine Lexi, and she named her doll, Sally. I made her angry when I told her that Sally wasn't a Black name. She in turn made me mad by saying, "I think the lighter dolls are prettier than these so I don't care what I name her."

My mouth flew open so fast, "Momma, Shay says the darker dolls aren't pretty, she likes the lighter ones because they are prettier. She doesn't like the doll you gave her!"

I remember my mother opening the screen door so hard I thought it would come off of the hinges. Before we knew it she was on the front porch with us sternly speaking.

Mom, "I'm going to say this and I'm going to say it only one time, do you hear me?"

In unison we both replied, "Yes, ma'am."

She continued. "Don't you ever, and I do mean *ever* let me hear you say that someone is prettier or better than the person you see in the mirror, do you hear me?"

Shay appeared frightened, as though she expected a spanking to come, but that was hardly the case. Plus, I really don't think a spanking would have pounded on us harder than my mother's words did. She went on a ten minute rant about Shay's comment. It seemed to come from a place of pain for my mother, though I never got the story behind it. At one point she made us both hold one of our lighter colored dolls next to the darker ones and tell her what was prettier one from the other.

Shay chose to stay quiet. I didn't make the initial comment so remained quiet, plus I thought they were both pretty. Mom went back in the house, and that was the end of that.

Let me say that Shay started off with the birth name of Sheila. Later in life she said Sheila didn't quite click with her and her personality. Eventually, she opted to go by the name of Shayla, unofficially, saying, "That has a better ring to it, it fits me better."

Before long she was down at the Hall of Records legally changing her name, not to Shayla, but to Shay, of course this didn't sit too well with her mother as she was named after a special aunt on her side of the family, but Shay didn't care.

Everywhere we went people often thought we were sisters, rather than first cousins; more often than not we didn't bother to correct them. We were oh so close. Most of our time together was spent at Gramby's house. This was the go-to place every weekend and all holidays where everyone met: aunts, uncles, cousins, friends, and any friends looking for any of my family members could find them there. It was also a place I *had to go*. Yes, I had to go with my mother every single weekend, whether I wanted to or not, well that is until I got a bit older and started asking if I could go bike riding with friends instead.

The highlight of going to Gramby's was that I'd see my favorite first cousin, Sheila I would hear her father's car pull up before I actually saw them. He had this ugly green clunker that made you wonder how they got to their destination, and better yet, if they'd make it home. I would nearly break my neck to get outside to see my favorite cousin. The weekends were brighter when Sheila was there. The holidays felt a bit more special when she was there. We'd curl up by Gramby's heater and teach ourselves how to crochet. We'd flip through the Right On magazines and look at the entertainers we were totally infatuated with. We'd just do girl stuff.

In time I noticed that Sheila didn't come anymore. Each time my uncle pulled up I would still break my neck outside and ask, "Where's Sheila?"

The response was the same for so long, that eventually I finally stopped asking.

"Oh she wanted to stay at her mother's."

It made me feel as though she didn't find the paternal side of her family important anymore.

By the time we were in our late twenties it seemed the relationship/ closeness was nonexistent, so much so I'll admit I felt some type of way when we finally reconnected again and learned she'd been married twice. All I could think was wow, two marriages, two bridal showers, and your first cousin couldn't make the invite lists.

Each time Shay came back around after playing Casper for months, even years, she would often have the same ol' line.

Shay, "We need to all get together and go out to eat like we used to do when we were younger."

In total shock that she even said it, all I could muster up in response was, "Well we do get together all the time, we never stopped, you're just not there. But as usual, you crawl from underneath whatever rock you've been under, and start coming back around for a couple of months, call more, visit more, then disappear for years again, but yes, the family gets together often, like I said, you're just not there."

In recent years Shay had been present more, but she was quite different, and don't get me wrong "different" isn't always a bad thing. But her "different" was something I didn't like being around. Shay carried around this new person with her who had this attitude of I'm better than everyone. It didn't take long to see why the friends she used to have were long gone. Let's face it; no one wants to be around that type of nonsense.

Though we weren't raised this way, Shay had this type of attitude now where she thought the world revolved around her. Her nose was turned up so high I'm surprised it didn't knock down a cloud or two. She was always clad in Gucci and Louis Vuitton, including accessories. She looked stunning all the time. But, she'd also become that person who always had to tell you what designer brand she was wearing, and how much it costed. "Oh this watch was only $3500 dollars."

With me being a bit more conservative than Shay, of course my mind would quickly venture to all the things I would buy with $3500, definitely not just one watch.

It was so difficult to be around her. I fell for the "Favorite First Cousin" role for a while, but eventually that was a boat I couldn't row anymore. Uncle James (Shay's dad) told me a couple of years before his passing, "Please stick close to Shay, you're all she has."

I honestly don't think he really knew what he was asking. As much as I love family, and as much as I adored being around her when we were younger, today is a new day. My mother and Uncle James hated when I'd tell them, "I have friends who are closer to me than some of my cousins, especially Shay, will ever be."

"Don't say that, blood is thicker than water."

"Yeah, that's what you guys say; I say, *Family is not always in the bloodline.*"

"Girl family is all you've got. Family is everything."

I believed that to a certain extent, with certain family members, but

I also know that family can sometimes be your biggest headache and can use you up, that is, if you let them.

Shay always hated the amount of friends I have who call me their sister, and they call me that for several reasons. Some…well I'm just that close to them, so anytime in their presence you'll surely hear them say, "Heeeey Sis." Others, well some (like me) don't have a sister and adopted me as such. But most are my sisters in Christ. Some of us have had conversations that Shay and I will never have. We've shared secrets Shay and I will never share. We've gone places and spent more time together than I would ever allow with this new Shay. And while Mom hates me to say this, it's true, except for the family bloodline, Shay and I wouldn't have a thing in common and probably wouldn't even be friends. I really believe that.

Oh don't get me wrong, I feel I've tried my very best to spend time with Shay and keep some type of family bond going, if for nothing else, I hear my uncle's voice, "You're all she has," but truly an hour with Shay feels like ten hours. There are some people you can be around and time moves too fast, and when it's time to part ways you're not ready, you want more. You wonder where the time went; you think of that old cliché, *time flies when you're having fun.* Kind of like the time I went to lunch with my long lost friend, Dawn. There we arrived at the restaurant at noon for lunch, only to find dinner guests arriving later. We had been in the restaurant talking and laughing so long, we'd totally lost track of time.

And of course there are people who you can be around and time seems to stand still, it just doesn't move fast enough. You look up at the clock and it says 12:30 p.m., and you look at the clock again and it says 12:35 p.m., time just isn't moving fast enough. Well, Shay would be in that category.

Mom and Uncle James are of the opinion that you deal with family come hell or high water, and I'm of the opinion that anyone negative, whether family or otherwise, I don't have to be around. I think some people call it, *loving them from a distance.*

Cousin Shay is that person who has one interest, one conversation, one concern, one priority, one thing she gets excited about, and that's SHAY. That's it, that's all, nothing else. If it's not about Shay, and if it's not for Shay, she's not the least bit interested, and quite honestly she doesn't even try to act as though she's interested. If by chance, and I do mean by chance a conversation makes its way onto another topic, Shay is just like the good ol' navigation system in the car, re-routing the conversation right back to her favorite topic...SHAY!!! It's beyond her to sit and listen to a conversation that concerns or holds the interest of someone else.

Shay's the one who can't have the eye liner the least bit crooked. She can't have a hair out of place. The make-up has to be perfect and refreshed all day. If the purse is black, the shoes will be too. Me, I want to look nice, and I do, believe me I do look nice every time I walk out of the house, but if I don't have time to change a purse so be it. If a strand falls out of my bun, I'm good. Plus, I think a strand falling out of the side of a bun is not monumental; as a matter of fact it looks cute. I think a broken nail today can wait until my appointment later in the week. It's not a 911 emergency to me. Oh, I'm not saying there's something wrong with being put-together, I'm just saying it really isn't the end of the world if you have a day or two where you're not.

It was quite funny one day when Shay joined me at the beach to walk. I explained to her that I power walk when I go to the beach, it's not about being cute, it's about working out. I could tell she didn't plan to break a sweat by what she was wearing. Of course she explained to me that she only wore Gucci active wear. The funny part was her reaction to what I had on. She appeared disgusted, though I thought I looked rather cute. My colors were coordinated; I was finally able to find some tall workout pants that didn't stop at my ankles. I matched them up with some nice workout attire. I slid my orthotics in my new tennis shoes, since the doctor required I wear them for lengthy walks, and I was good to go.

Shay, "You're not wearing that are you?"

Rather bewildered, I asked, "Why not?"

Appearing nauseated, Shay replied, "Please tell me you don't mix labels like that!"

I hadn't a clue what she was talking about until of course she explained it. I would then learn that my tall Xersion workout pants from JC Penney, coupled with my New Balance tennis shoes, coupled with my Nike shirt, and Adidas jacket were driving her crazy. Although everything matched and was well color coordinated, with black and purple, the fact that they were different designers broke some rule.

"Brooklyn, you don't mix designer labels like that. If you have on Nike, everything needs to be Nike. If you have on Jordan's, everything has to be Jordan's. You don't do that."

Quite emphatically I responded, "I do. Are you ready to go?"

I thought that was the funniest thing I'd ever heard. So now in addition to making sure my color scheme matches I'm supposed to worry about labels. Not happening.

Another annoying characteristic of Shay is that she always has a story that one-ups someone else's. If this person is telling a story of something they've done and experienced firsthand in their own life, Shay has another story that minimizes that person's story, and even discounts the validity of their story, even though they've experienced it. She's the one always interrupting, "Wait, Wait, Wait, let me say this, oh I've got to tell you guys this before I forget," as though no one was talking, totally drowning out the person who was talking, totally burglarizing the conversation.

Have you ever been around someone who has to have the floor in all conversations? Someone who always knows more about every subject even though they've never experienced it and you have; but can tell you how the process goes; always has to upstage the next person. Well if you haven't, let me introduce you to Shay. Yes, Ms. Shay McGlover. I'll tell you she's going to have the better story and the last word even if she has to make something up. I'll never forget the time she interjected into a conversation as Ro was telling a few of us about her vacation, Shay totally took the wheel. Ro stood there with a look on her face that read, *I thought I was talking*. But there went Shay, "Oh I just got back from Venice, it's beautiful."

I couldn't believe it. I rolled my eyes and thought oh here she goes again. Everyone oooh and ahhh'd as she described Venice, Italy.

Keisha said, "Oh my God, I've always wanted to go to Venice, that's on my bucket list."

Shay continued, "Girl it's absolutely beautiful, and so clean. The architect of the buildings is breathtaking."

She went on and on about Venice, Italy, telling about all the beautiful landmarks, the beautiful churches, the Grand Canal, and so forth. She elaborated on things as though she knew much about it. She sounded as one who was well-traveled, yet I knew she hated to fly, so much so there had been times when we were younger where Shay opted to drive hours to a destination than board a plane.

But, there she was telling everyone of her trip to Venice, Italy, and with much excitement I might add. She told everyone her favorite points of interests being Riviera del Brenta, Ponte di Rialto, and St. Mark's Square. I wondered why she felt she always had to steal the show, instead of letting others have the floor sometimes.

I imagine she'd read up on Venice, Italy quite a bit to know so much about it, she appeared to know more about it than others at the table who had vacationed there before. But, truth be told Shay has only been to Venice, CA, not Venice, Italy. It made me think of a guy I read about many years ago who told women he had attended Penn State, when in fact he had been in the State Penn, a bit of a twist on words like Shay does.

In addition to being that person who always has to steal the show, have the last word, one-up everyone, Shay…well this new Shay, is also rude, abrupt and short with people. A gentle greeting from a stranger on the street is met with much negativity.

"Good Morning."

"What's so good about it?"

"How are you today?"

Her response to that question (that is, if she answers) is, "What do you care how I'm doing today, you don't even know me?"

Often I'd be left standing there in amazement just as the person who greeted her would be, both speechless wondering how a simple kind gesture of greeting a stranger went bad. Yet there were times I would address the issue with Shay asking her if it was really necessary to be rude to someone who took the time to acknowledge her. Of course that never went well.

"Brooklyn, I don't need anyone to acknowledge me. How about you respond to people the way you want to respond to them, and I'll respond the way I want to. I don't see why someone is asking me how I'm doing in the first place. Okay, so what if I responded that I wasn't doing well, what are they going to do about it?"

I would again ask Shay how and why she changed so much, also adding, "It's common courtesy Shay."

"That's what you're missing Brooklyn, I don't care how they're doing so I don't ask. What do I care how someone I've never met is doing?"

It all reminded me of the times Shay and I would be out together and I'd see Jackie, a homeless lady who sits in front of 7-Eleven, and after sharing a few words with her I'd hand her a few dollars.

"Girl please, if I have to get up and go to work every day, they can, too. I ain't passing out any of my money to anyone who chooses to go sit in front of 7-Eleven every day, or make a street sign and stand on a corner, or better yet, have you seen all these women with their kids in the grocery store parking lots nowadays, that one lady was proven not even to be pregnant? Do you really think that two dollars you gave that woman is going to change her homeless situation?"

I replied, "No, probably not, but it probably made her feel good just to be acknowledged. You've changed so much Shay."

"Well people change, and I'm proof of that. People are always talking about change is good right, well guess what? I've changed."

"Obviously. Where did you get this rude attitude from? You act like the world revolves around you."

"Who else should it revolve around?"

"Girl please. I'm serious. You're always walking around like you're sucking on lemons, you're mean to everyone, mad at everyone. There has to be a time when you have at least one good day Shay! And, while we're talking did you have to say what you said to Taja last week?"

"What?"

"You don't have any filters Shay, you say what you want and never think of the other person."

"Oh you mean I don't stop to sugar coat everything like you do? I can't even remember what I said. What did I say?"

"Girl please, you do your crap and then always get amnesia. You remember and I know you remember, Taja was telling us about the headaches she'd been having and you had to tell her about Uncle Ty."

"Well it's the truth, he was having headaches too and he died. Did I lie? He died, didn't he? All I told her was that she probably had a tumor like Uncle Ty."

I never quite understood the insensitive nature of people in situations like this, and I've seen it so many times where someone knows a person is going through a medical condition themselves, and they choose to share with them the darkest stories about someone in a similar situation. "Oh my aunt was fourth stage cancer, too, and she died, you normally don't come back from fourth stage cancer."

Really? Why not tell someone a different story, why not tell them about the people you know who had fourth stage cancer and beat it? Why not shed some positive to the situation, instead of a woe story? Why not encourage them in the fight?

"Can you muster up something positive sometimes? Everything is negative unless it's about you Shay. The only time you light up is when you're talking about yourself. There have been times when you could easily give another beautiful young lady a compliment, but instead of being kind enough to take that opportunity you flip it to you again, of course."

"What are you talking about now Brooklyn?"

I went on to share with Shay all the times she looks at other women and has nothing good to say, she can never extend a compliment to someone else. It's either, "She thinks she looks cute." Or, "That dress would look better on me."

"You know she heard what you said."

"I don't care, I said what I meant, it would look better on me."

"You know Shay, sometimes you don't have to say anything at all. You don't have to comment on everything, you don't have to critique everyone, it's okay to just be quiet, and it actually works out better sometimes. Was it too hard to say, "I love your outfit, you look very nice." How about make someone else's day sometimes Shay, it's not always about you."

"It is always about me."

"And, I noticed you always have to say whatever you say very loud, loud enough for the person you're talking about to hear it. You have no regard for anyone's feelings. You know that lady heard every word you said about her dress and how it would look better on you."

"And?"

"And, it needs to stop Shay. You know what I also get tired of?"

"What now Brooklyn?"

"Every time you talk about someone, and tell me to look their direction they think I'm just as messy and rude as you are, when in fact I haven't opened my mouth. The attitude Shay is why your friends aren't around anymore. No one wants to deal with and be around that type of attitude all the time. It's like you go to bed mad and wake up mad, too. What is that? How can someone walk around mad at everything and everyone every single day? People get tired of the complaining and condescending comments towards them. It's like you made this choice to be mad all the time."

She shrugged her shoulders.

I had a male friend once tell me, "I think if someone walked up to your cousin and handed her a million dollars she'd still be mad. I can hear her now asking, with much attitude, why it was given to her."

We buckled over in laughter at that moment, but it's really not funny. Another friend, Ed, used to always say, "You know if your cousin would work on the inside as much as she does the outside she'd be one bad sister. She's got one nasty attitude. Mac can't cover up ugly on the inside. I speak to that girl every time I see her and she won't part her lips, not a nod, nothing. Will it kill her to speak?"

Sometimes I would take the time to talk to Shay about her attitude when people shared their comments with me, but of course that fell on deaf ears.

Her normal response was, "Girl, people are jealous of me, and that's the bottom line. If a female says something about me it's because they are mad because they don't look this good, and if a male says it it's because he can't get with this. When you have it going on you'll have haters, that's how it works Brook, haters hate, if they didn't hate they couldn't be called haters, right?"

But, for now, at this very present moment, Shay was standing at my door unannounced and there was nothing I could do but speak.

"Hey." I was trying to make my outer response more pleasant than what I was feeling inside, still upset with myself that I went back and checked the stove ten times. If the stove was off the first time, then it was still off.

"What's all that singing about, I heard you all the way out here?"

I chose not to answer her question because it was so much like Shay to come at me with that type of approach. And, do I really need to break down an explanation as to why I was singing. Why do people sing?

"Where are you headed so early? I see you're not responding to any texts."

"My mom just left, and I didn't hear my phone."

I honestly hadn't heard my cell phone, had I heard it I would have answered it to divert Shay's visit this morning.

"What's your t-shirt say?"

I turned to let her see it, but was still annoyed with myself.

She read it aloud, "P.U.S.H. – PRAY UNTIL SOMETHING HAPPENS."

She continued, "Girl please, with all the stuff you've been through I don't know if I'd trust that prayer thing. You might want to put on another shirt."

Amused, she continued, "So tell me, how long do you have to pray til' something happens?"

In irritation I ignored her because it was so much like Shay to try to ruin someone's day. I didn't feel like it. She always seemed to find pleasure in stirring the pot. Fortunately, I've learned to ignore her.

"Where are you headed? "

"I have no specific destination, just hanging out, going wherever I choose. No order, no concrete plans, I just want to get out of this house. I'm so glad it's the weekend. It's absolutely beautiful out here. Great job God!"

She rolled her eyes.

"With who?"

"Huh?"

"Who are you going with?"

"No one, going out alone today, that's what I feel like, and that's what I'm doing. I think I'm going to start at the beach and walk a few miles, and then probably take myself to lunch or something, I've been craving some of that shrimp ravioli from the Italian place I like on Lincoln, and those garlic balls are to die for."

"I don't see what you like about that place."

I kept a blank stare, still wishing she wasn't on my porch.

She continued, "The food isn't all that good to me. I remember when Blake took me there and I just about died. I couldn't believe he took me to that cheap place, I think each of our plates were fifteen dollars. He had the wrong person with that one. You need to spend a whole lot more on me than fifteen dollars if you want my time, especially on a first date. Actually I don't normally get up to get dressed if you aren't taking me to some place waaaaay more upscale than that. Fifteen dollars? Girl please, my breakfasts cost more than that. If a man can't take me somewhere I can't afford to take myself, then I don't need him. I guess you would be okay with that place on a first date?"

"Yep, second, third and all of the other dates, too. I don't have a problem with it. Obviously the food is good; you can hardly get inside the place, every time I go, or pass by there's a line spilling outside of the building. Plus if it's someone you want to be with does it really matter how much it cost?"

My words appeared to shock Shay, "Yeah, it sure does matter. I'm worth way more than that."

"Okay, so now you're basing your value on what a meal cost?"

She chose not to answer me, finally she was quiet, and it appeared I was now irritating her, and to be honest I was happy to see the roles had reversed.

"Shay, I'd rather eat a happy meal in a beautiful park with someone I wanted to be with, than a steak dinner with someone I don't at some fancy schmancy restaurant."

"Well that's you, and you can do just that because like I said he had the wrong person with that one, taking me to that cheap place."

I stood watching her mouth constantly move, wondering how someone could talk that much. I couldn't believe her level of ungratefulness, and entitlement. She was overwhelming. I wondered if people who complained all the time knew just how difficult it was to be around them. I wondered if they heard themselves complain or if it's so normal they don't realize how much they complain, but then I paused and figured if they were anything like Shay they really didn't care.

"He had the nerves to keep asking me if I liked the food, showed me the awards on the walls the restaurant had received throughout the years. I was not impressed in the least, with all the crooked stuff people do these days they can create their own awards on the computer, and hang them up, and I bet that's what they did."

"Yeah, that's something you would think Shay. You always think the negative."

By the time Shay finished ranting and raving about a restaurant I liked, of which I hadn't invited her to in the first place, I was ready for her to go.

Shay, "Why don't we hang out today? And we can go to the Italian restaurant I like. I'll pay."

"No I'm good Shay. I don't need you to pay, I have money. But, I can't do it today. My nerves can't handle it. I'm going to hit the beach and knock off a few other things on my list, and go wherever my car leads me, I don't feel like all of the nonsense today."

She had the nerves to ask me, "What nonsense?"

"What nonsense?"

"Yeah."

"The drama you drag around with you everywhere you go these days, I don't feel like it today. I can't do it Shay. It's draining. I just want to *do me*. I don't feel like all the talk about why I shop at this store, and how it's low budget, and how I should go to this store and that store, when I am quite fine shopping at the stores I shop at, you're the only one who has a problem with where I shop."

Shay hated that I loved Macy's so much, and how I loved to go into their Last Act section and look for all the bargains. It was exciting to me to find a $200 dress marked down to $29. In excitement I would snap a picture of the tag or the receipt and send it to my girlfriends who shared my same fascination with bargains, "How's this for a deal?"

The last time it was such a good deal Evette responded, "Girl you better hurry up and start the car and get out of there before they realize they made a mistake on that tag."

Shay hated that I had no problem going through TJ Maxx and Marshalls looking for bargains.

"Brooklyn, when you shop at places like that you're going to see others in the same thing you have on."

"And?"

"And, who wants to look like everyone else?"

"Shay, I've been shopping at those stores for years, and can't tell you one time I've come across someone who had on the same thing I did, and guess what? I wouldn't care if I did."

"Well, I like to shop at the higher-end stores that don't make things in bulk, or I'll get the tailor to make me a few pieces. But, let's hang today, we can stop and get a massage, we haven't hung out in a while. Let's do the Fountain View Mall, because the other mall doesn't have anything in there for me but an Exit Sign. I'll pay for your massage."

"I'm good Shay. I can pay for my own massage. I actually love the mall I'm going to, and the guy, Paul, in the massage place there is off the chain, so I'm good."

"How do you go to those massage places in the mall?"

"Easy. I walk in; tell them I want an hour back massage, and a thirty minute foot massage, lay on the table, pay and leave, that's how."

"They're so low budget, and none of the frills of the place I go to."

"Like I said Shay, you go where you want to go, and I'm going where I want to go. I love it there. Paul is awesome. I don't have one complaint, and I don't need some cucumbers in my water, and a robe to make me feel as though I've gotten better service."

"So we aren't hanging out today?"

"No I'm good Shay. I woke up wanting a drama free day, and that's exactly what I'm going to have."

I wanted to tell Shay I was guarding my peace, but that would have turned into a whole different conversation and I was ready to go.

I motioned for Shay to move further off the porch so that I could close my door. "Move Shay, I'm about to get out of here."

She continued talking, "Oh wait a minute, I know what this is about. Are you serious; are you still mad at what happened the last time we hung out?"

"I'm not mad at anything. I've come to know my limits of what I can take and what I don't want to be bothered with, and more so what I don't *have to* deal with, that's it, that's all. I've had a pretty hectic workweek, I woke up feeling great, and ready for a peaceful day, and that's exactly what I'll have…a peaceful day. I can't do the drama today. Move so I can close the door."

In that moment I thought about something someone posted on Facebook earlier in the week, and yes it made me think of Shay, then, and now as she stood before me, *Sometimes you just have to be done, not mad, not upset, JUST DONE!* And that's where I was, done!

"Drama? You're saying I'm drama?"

"I'm learning to protect my peace Shay."

"Protect your peace, whatever that means?"

"Think about it. I'll explain it to you one day, but I need you to back up some so I can close and lock this door, I'm getting out of here. I don't have to remind you how the last outing we had turned out, and that was the last straw for me."

"See I knew you were still mad at that."

"I'm not mad; but we're not hanging out today. It ain't happening."

Honestly, I swore if the good Lord got me home the last time I spent a day with Shay, I would not put myself in a situation like that again. It was the longest day ever, and I wasn't giving up this beautiful Saturday morning to take a chance at experiencing that again, and allowing this day to go sideways.

"Every time we go somewhere Shay I find myself apologizing for something you've said or done, and I'm tired of it. The comment you made to Mrs. Griffin the last time we hung out together was totally unnecessary. It was a shot below the belt."

"I don't need anyone apologizing for me. Plus I don't remember what happened."

"Shay, please don't act like you don't remember what happened that day. *Everything* happened that day, and it was totally unnecessary, to be honest with you, it was evil."

"What?"

"Here you go with that amnesia again. Shay that lady is 75 years old, show some respect. Mrs. Griffin was part of our village growing up. Things weren't like they are today, we respected our elders. We *had* to treat her and any other adult with the same respect we gave our own parents; otherwise it would be hell to pay from them and our parents. It's not like it is today where a lot of parents don't want you to say anything to their kids. She was a big part of our village growing up."

"Village?"

"Yes, she was a part of our village. It takes a village Shay, and she was a part of ours."

"She didn't do anything for me."

"Yeah, okay, believe that if you want to, your memory loss is something else. But, if you'd look back a lot of our school supplies and clothes came from her, and don't forget all the Christmas and birthday gifts. She treated us as if we were her own. She only had boys and always wanted girls, so we benefited greatly from it."

"Whatever."

"Okay, so things didn't work out in your marriage to Jackson, but he had just passed away Shay, and you knew she was hurting when we saw her at the mall that day, but what you said was totally rude and uncalled for, and she's never done anything to you. It's as though you wait for chances to get hurtful digs into people. Shoot, I credit her with helping me be the lady I am today, yes indeed, big time. She helped to instill some really good foundation in us."

Shay rolled her eyes, "Speak for yourself."

"Your rudeness that day was really hard to believe. It showed me how much you've changed, because the old Shay would have never been so cruel. It showed me just how low you will go."

"Well she's the one who asked if we would be attending Jackson's service."

"No Shay, she asked me if I would be attending the service, but you chimed in with your two cents, instead of staying out of our conversation."

"Well it's the truth, I told her the truth. What is it, people can't tell the truth anymore, or does everyone have to be…"

She couldn't collect her thoughts so was searching for the words. When she found them she flailed her arms in the air and said, "Oh I got it, I'm not politically correct. Is that it Brooklyn? I can't tell the truth because it's not politically correct, right Brook? It's not sugar coated enough!"

I sighed.

She continued, "I told her exactly what I wanted to tell her, that the only reason I'd be at the service was to make sure he was in the casket."

"And you think that was right?"

"It was the truth. It was right to me. The only reason I'd go to his service is to see for myself that he was in that box, that's it, that's all. You surely won't see me grabbing for a tissue when the ushers come by. Oh excuse me…did I say that right? Or, is it "ursher" as the good ol' church folk say?" She laughed.

"Well, you see she paid you absolutely no attention at all, although I know it hurt her, because you made a point to make sure she heard every word you said. You saw her expression change. Have you noticed everyone has grown except you Shay? Did you hear her response to your rude comment?"

"No."

"That's because she didn't respond, she didn't even give you the satisfaction of a response, didn't pay you or what you said any attention. You know why?"

"Why?"

"She didn't respond because it's not worth it to respond to ignorance."

All she said *to me*, not you was, "Well, I'm 75 years old, and I've been trusting the Lord a long time, and He's got a pretty good track record of not making mistakes. I was told Jackson wouldn't live past eight years of age, yet I had him forty more years than that. I'm grateful. Oh, we're not ever ready to say goodbye to a loved one, much less a child, but I'm grateful to have had him all the years I did. All I know is we can't take all the sunshine life gives us and not expect to get rained on sometimes, too. It hurts right now, my God does it ever hurt, but I'm gonna keep trusting Him."

Shay barked, "And you told me that story because you thought I wanted to hear it?"

"No, I was just showing you how you hurt people Shay. As they say, hurt people hurt people. Look I can't do the Negative Nelly and Debbie Downer today, I'm out of here."

With much sarcasm Shay told me, "I like the way you asked her if there was anything you could do for her for the service."

"What's wrong with that?"

"Just seems to me since I'm your cousin you wouldn't have done that."

"Wow Shay…you know that's another thing you need to get out of, you expect folks to dislike whoever you dislike and it doesn't work like that. Plus it seems you hate everyone."

"Whatever. Are you really going to let her put you on the program like that?"

"Yes, I told her I would do whatever she needed me to do, and nothing you say will change that. I'll be stopping by her house later today to see what she needs. You know Shay; if you were honest you'd have to admit Jackson was a really good man."

"Please don't go there."

I motioned for Shay to move again, "Come on, stop playing, I'm ready to leave. I'm really leaving now. I'm not going to stand here all day talking."

"I'm going with you Brook."

"No you're not Shay. You were rude to everyone you came in contact with the last time we spent the day together, and I'm not doing it. As though the rudeness to Mrs. Griffin wasn't enough, you had to say something to the young lady parking in the handicap spot, as though you know her medical condition. You couldn't park there yourself anyway, so why get involved? And, then you had the audacity to ask that saleslady about her hair."

"And, what was wrong with that? All I asked her was, "Why do you ladies allow those hairstylists to keep putting those braids and weaves in your hair, your hairline is now behind your ear, your hair may never grow back?"

"You hurt her feelings Shay. And what if...let's say just maybe her hair situation was due to some medical condition and you did that to her?"

Shay laughed, "Girl please, you know that wasn't a medical condition, and if it is a medical condition then a whole bunch of women have that same condition of no more hairline. But, I know what it is."

"What is it Shay?"

"Oh I'll tell you exactly what it is, it's a bunch of money hungry stylist still sewing and gluing hair in folk's heads when they can see the hair has broken off. Ching, Ching...yeah that's all they care about is the money. Well it's the truth. They see one little strand left, and they'll glue something on to that, too. So you've never looked around and seen all these ladies with a hairline that starts behind their ears? Yep, the hairline is now clear at the middle of their heads, and some of em' try to pull out baby hair like Gramby used to do with our hair when we were kids, but the difference is *we were kids* and we had baby hair, but that ain't baby hair, that's broken off hair that ain't growing back. And do you see how early they're starting these little girl's weaves and extensions? They don't stand a chance, they're gonna look just like their mothers, bald. Girl don't tell me you haven't seen it?"

"Yeah I've seen it Shay. I see it every day, but it's their head!! All I'm saying Shay is you constantly concentrate on the outside of people. That young lady was one of the best sales reps I've ever had, but you couldn't compliment her on that. You couldn't thank her for the excellent service she provided? It's too much to lift someone else up Shay, huh? It's too hard to make someone else's day."

"I guess it is."

"You know, perhaps when we left the store you could have just mentioned it to me, but did you have to say something to her? And, to answer your question again, I do see everything you see, I see the beautiful females who tattoo their faces now, I see folks without hair lines, I see the green, blue, purple hair, I see a whole bunch of stuff, but do I approach everyone Shay? No. And by the way, you don't know where that conversation could have gone when you approached that girl with the tattoos on her face that day. It could have gotten really ugly. All I can say is maybe one day you'll learn that some things can go unsaid, and also you might learn that it's not always what you say, but how you say it."

"Oh I feel another sermon coming on."

That was Shay's favorite line when she was tired of hearing what I was saying, or her other favorite word, "*Whatever.*"

I could tell Shay felt some type of way about the decline of her offer to hang out, but though it was a long time coming, in recent months I'd finally learned to say no to people, and while it took a little longer with Shay, I was finally there with her as well. I'd finally learned to stop filling my weekends with stuff I didn't want to do, causing me to return to work on Mondays feeling as though I hadn't had a weekend myself, because I did everything everyone else wanted me to do, and nothing I wanted to do. But, I'd finally learned, and while I noticed some folks felt some type of way about it, I didn't. If after a long week of working I didn't feel like sitting at yet another girlfriend's child's baby shower, then I didn't. If I didn't feel like going to yet another jewelry party, I didn't. I finally got waaaaay past getting upset when certain invitations didn't come my way. I've played enough clothes pin games, don't cross this and that, unscramble these words, to last me a lifetime.

And, if I didn't wish to go shopping with Shay, I didn't. Unlike me Shay didn't seem to have a budget, and that's well and good. Her shopping and spending seemed to be way out of my league, and there's nothing like going shopping with someone who grabs everything they want without hesitation and you're making sure to stay on a budget. I always seemed to turn into Shay's caddy, carrying all of her bags around. Oh don't get me wrong, I feel I've done well for myself, but I do have a stopping point, and I definitely do have a budget. I do have to watch what I spend, apparently Shay doesn't. Hats off to her if she has it like that, I know Uncle James left her some money, but I don't think he left that much because he always told Shay, "If you don't change that attitude of entitlement you have, and get that big boulder off your shoulder I'm not leaving you anything."

As I backed my car out of the driveway, I could hear Shay, "I'll be good today, I'll be nice, can I go with you?"

"I'm good Shay. Talk to you later." I hit the accelerator looking forward to a peaceful day where I didn't have to apologize to anyone for Shay's comments or actions. I didn't have to tell anyone, "I'm sorry, that's just how she is." I didn't have to explain to anyone why I liked this store, or restaurant, or hear her telling me how disgusting it was that I liked stopping at yard sales, "Who wants someone else's junk?"

One thing about life is that we all have choices. And with that said, if Shay chooses to be the way she is, I can choose not to be around it. Choices. I rolled back my sunroof and exhaled, enjoying the fact that there was nothing in my passenger seat except my purse.

I found myself humming, nearly skipping enjoying being out and about, without anyone saying, "Do you really like that? I don't like that. I know you're not buying that. Whew, I hope no one sees me stopping at this yard sale with you, couldn't you have dropped me off first." What a great day! Peaceful! Relaxing! Drama free!

After eating at the Italian restaurant of my choice, I waited for the bill only to be told a gentleman across the way at another table had covered it. I caught him as he walked out of the restaurant and thanked him.

"I saw you over there by yourself and I wanted to pay it forward in paying your tab. I didn't want to interrupt your lunch. I saw you nodding to music; you looked as though you were at peace, something my life is totally lacking right now."

"Oh you could have interrupted me, but you're right, I was listening to "Healing Song" by Greg Karukas. Yeah, I was in a different zone. Good food, good music, can't beat that."

"Yeah, you're right. It's a small gesture, but it was placed on my heart to do it."

"Actually it's not a small gesture at all. Honestly you don't know just how BIG of a gesture it is, honestly it's huge. You don't see a lot of kind gestures in this world today. Thank you."

"Well it's not like you ordered a whole lot to break the bank or anything, but it's something I wanted to do."

"Doesn't matter how much you spent; I'll take the gift from the heart over money any day. Do you mind if I hug you?"

I reached to hug this stranger, "I'm Brooklyn."

He told me his name was Andre. "Thank you so much for paying for my lunch, you didn't have to do that, nor pay for the extra meal I ordered for tomorrow. I guess you never know who's watching you. I pray whatever peace you saw in me today, you find it in your life."

Andre replied, "Me, too. What's that little grin on your face?"

"Oh nothing, you made me think of something my grandmother used to say."

"What's that?"

"Peace doesn't mean there's no noise in your life. It just means your heart is calm as you ride out the storm."

"Thanks. I needed that. Hopefully I'll see you here again."

"I'm sure you will."

I had one more stop to make before heading home. I pulled into Mrs. Griffin's driveway as I always did, as though I lived there. I did the normal two taps on the door, and commenced to open the door. I found her at the dining room table dabbing her eyes as she went through some pictures.

"Did I catch you at a bad time?"

"There's no such thing as a bad time when it comes to you baby girl. I was having a moment; I suppose I'll have many more of those. Thank God for all these memories left behind. I'll tell you some of these pictures I'm going through have made me laugh so hard I cried, and others just made me cry, but it's going to be alright."

She reached for a stack of pictures, "Look at this one here, that boy loved to play in his church clothes for some reason, now if he had on play clothes he would have been sitting his tail on the porch, but here he has on a suit and rolling in the grass. He must've been about ten years old on this one." She laughed.

She continued, "Girl look at this one, he hardly had any teeth in his mouth here. I remember having to get a knife to cut his corn off the cob because he had no teeth in the front to bite into it."

She had one of those laughs where her whole upper body shook when she laughed. She also had one of those laughs where she cried, totally bursting in laughter and wiping tears at the same time. But, this time the tears were for Jackson.

"Look at this one, we bought him all those toys for Christmas, and here he is playing with the box the fire truck came in all day, never once did he play with the fire truck, just the box. My goodness, that's my boy."

She reached over and took my hand. I looked down at her hand on top of mine and for the first time noticed all the wrinkles. I gently put my other hand on top of hers and we were both silent. I don't know what she was thinking in her silence, but I thought about all the years those hands of hers lifted me up off the pavement when I fell; all the times she spanked us neighborhood kids; all the times those hands cooked a meal when my mother was late coming home; all the times I felt those hands pulling the covers over me at night when she didn't want to wake me up when my parents were late. I even thought about how no other woman, except my own mother, could say "It's going to be alright," and make you believe it... even in adulthood, like she could.

I broke the silence, "I was headed home and wanted to get whatever you had for me to read at the service."

"You sure you don't mind doing this?"

"No ma'am, I don't mind." Honestly I did mind, but didn't have the heart to tell her I couldn't do it. I was hoping she'd give me some poem or acknowledgements to read, but that wasn't the case. She wanted me to read his life story.

"Here you go baby, I don't know why they read these things at services anyway, you know folks read it as soon as the ushers hand them one, but his kids want it read so that's that. Oh wait a minute, only seven people will be chosen to speak, did you want to say anything?"

"Thank you. If you don't mind I think reading about his life will be difficult enough to get through."

"I'm glad they are designating and limiting the speakers. Gotta love them folks who get up there to say a few words and go into some horrible rendition of Amazing Grace, when they weren't asked to sing in the first place. Or the ones who try to go well over the specified time talking about, "Wait a minute I just have a couple more things to say.""

We laughed. She dabbed her eyes.

"You're funny. I'm just glad you're able to find some light moments during this time."

"Yeah but you know I'm telling the truth. I just hope none of that nonsense happens at his service. The kids wanted everyone to wear his favorite color, but I don't know who came up with all that crazy stuff for funerals where people wear certain colors, but I just want to get my baby buried. I have more to concern myself with than everyone being color coordinated. Well, you know this is all for us anyway, cause he's long gone. But I would like to just get what remains of him buried. My, my, my, what a son he was. He was surely a momma's boy. He sure took care of me."

"I hear you. Alright I'll see you at the service, if the Lord says the same."

"Baby girl, that's been your favorite saying for years, but it's the truth. You know I always wondered why my son didn't end up with you."

"Stop it. Oh here you go again, let me get out of here. And before I leave, please allow me to apologize for Shay and her cruel words when we saw you that day. It was rude and totally lacked any compassion. You know we weren't raised that way, of course you know we weren't raised that way because you helped raise us."

"Oh I know."

"So believe me, I know better, and she knows better to talk to you that way. I'm so sorry."

"Don't be sorry sweetheart, you've been apologizing for her a long time now, it's fine. I just have to consider the source, that's definitely not the young lady I once knew, poised and so polite. But, she'll one day realize she has made her own storms in her life. Just maybe things will work out for her one day if she learns to get out of her own way. Enough stuff comes our way in life without us doing anything to cause it, but she'll learn one day, you can believe that. I've been around a long time and you can best believe we don't get away with anything in this life, nothing. Stuff catches up to you."

"Ok, I'm gonna go, unless there's anything else you need."

"I'm good baby girl, thank you."

"I love you…I love you more."

I smiled.

If you judge people, you have no time to love them.

While you were busy judging others, you left your closet door open and a lot of skeletons fell out.

A chip on the shoulder is too heavy a piece of baggage to carry through life.

Don't judge people, you never know what type of battle they are fighting.

Friendship is not about people who act true to your face. It's about people who remain true behind your back.

Best friends make the good times even better; and the hard times easier.

Friends know you, and love you just the same.

There are some people in life who make you laugh a little louder, and smile a little bigger.

CHAPTER

Two

"You can't do that Brooklyn."

"Why not Mom?"

"It's not right."

"How are you going to have a birthday party and not invite your only female first cousin on your father's side like that? You know that's not right, especially since you're inviting all of your cousins on my side, come on Brook, how is that going to look?"

"It's going to look like she wasn't invited."

"Oh now you're being sassy."

"No I'm not. I don't want to be bothered with her attitude mom. I don't get it, everyone else can have a party and invite whoever they want, but you're telling me I have to invite her. I don't want her negativity there. I don't want the attitude. She's always walking around with some chip on her shoulder, and I don't want that at my gathering. Do you remember she had two bridal showers and two weddings and we didn't see an invitation?"

"Yeah, I remember, but we don't do what others do, we try to handle things a bit differently. Brook, I may have missed the ball as a mother in some areas raising you; you didn't come with a manual you know, but I do believe I taught you right from wrong, didn't I?"

"Yes ma'am, and you are and have always been the perfect mother."

"You better had said that," while pinching my right cheek as though I was still her seven year old Brookie.

Deep...and I do mean very deep down inside I felt mom was right. How do you explain inviting nearly 50 ladies, and not Shay? I didn't think any of the other ladies at the birthday event would miss Shay at all, and I surely wouldn't, but while it was something I didn't want to do, it actually felt as though it was the right thing to do. I certainly didn't want to intentionally hurt Shay, I know she didn't care about other people's feelings, but I did. Hey, maybe I'll be lucky and she'll get the invitation and not attend.

"I'll think about it mom."

She shot one of those looks my way, kind of like the way she used to when I was little and acting up in church.

"Brooklyn!!!?"

"Alright. Alright. I'll do it. I'll invite her."

"And another thing, don't give her that much power to change the atmosphere of your party, how about you all let your lights shine so bright it overtakes her darkness. Shoot, maybe it will rub off on her. How about that? You ever think about that?"

"Yeah, how about that, mom? Okay, you win."

For more years than I could count I had forsaken what I wanted to do for my birthdays. I'd plan things with whoever I was dating at the time, and the plans would fall through, letting me know this day wasn't as important to him as it was to me. Then, there were those birthdays where friends constantly asked what I wanted to do for my birthday and I hadn't a clue, and the day simply passed by. And, of course those times when something needing to be repaired at the house or on the car robbed me of the birthday celebration I wanted, but things were different this year. I knew exactly what I wanted to do, and while it may not have all the glam and glitter that others may think it should have, I was tickled pink about it all. I didn't ponder or need an Option B or C as a backup plan, I was rolling with Option A, the only one I had.

Shay's response to hearing my birthday plans, "Are you kidding Brooklyn? I know you can do better than that for your 50th birthday. Please tell me you're kidding girl."

"I'm not kidding. I'm serious that's what I've really, really been wanting to do. I want a Girls In My Circle evening."

"A girls in your circle what?"

"Just an evening with girlfriends."

"Girl please, you can do that anytime."

"Yeah, we can, but we haven't so that's what I want."

"You're telling me that's all you can come up with? Of all the things you can do in Cali, that's all you've got? It sounds a bit uneventful to me."

I was pleased with my plans, and not Shay or anyone else would change it. It sounded good to me when it first came to my mind, and it sounded even better now. It was on my heart, and had been on my heart a long, long time. All I wanted was to dine with ladies who had walked this thing called life with me, women who all held some piece of the Brooklyn Puzzle of Life.

Perhaps Shay won't be the only person who thought this was corny, but it's what I wanted. I wanted to take it as far back as elementary school, to girls who were what Tracie Fisher calls, "sandbox friends." In today's lingo I would venture to say most had the title of BFF at different intervals in my life, and I wanted to celebrate life with them all for my 50th.

I wasn't going to worry about who showed up, or who liked the idea, this was what I wanted. Gramby used to say, "Don't ever concern yourself with the folks who don't come, just enjoy and love on the ones who do. Remember everyone who is there is who was *supposed* to be there, and took the time out of their schedules to attend, don't worry about the rest. If only one person shows up, you two enjoy yourselves and dance as though no one is watching."

Well I sure hoped more than one person showed up, but I understood Gramby's point.

"Brooklyn, who wants to spend they're 50th with a bunch of women? You know you only turn 50 once, you should really do it up."

"I don't know why people say that crazy stuff all the time."

"What?"

"That you only turn 50 once."

"Well it's true!"

"Yeah, but you only turn 25 once. You only turn 40 once. You only turn 50 once. Don't you turn every age just once? Tell me this, how many have you repeated?"

"I'm just saying it's a milestone and you should really do it up."

"Don't start Shay, it's my birthday remember. It's what I want. Just us.

No concern of who has a date and who doesn't. No attitudes. Just us all catching up and laughing."

"Well I don't do women like that."

"What do you mean you don't do women?"

"I just don't."

"Why's that? Do you feel intimidated when you're around other women?"

"Intimidated? Girl please. Now that's funny, you've got jokes huh? I just don't do women. I don't like being around other women, I don't like hanging with other women."

"Oh I get that sometimes we're not always nice to one another, and can do better loving on and building one another up, but you sure can't lump everyone in the same bag, surely there are some women you don't mind being around."

Speaking very slowing and precise as though I was hard of hearing, she repeated, "Did you hear me Brooklyn, I don't do women."

"I don't get that Shay, everything you've ever been through it's been women around you who helped you back up, so you need to lose that attitude. You don't do women!!!? Really Shay?"

"Yeah, really."

"Girl please, every single time your back was up against the wall, or you found your butt down in one of life's ditches it was the women in your life extending their arm to help pull you up. Same with me Shay, every time life got a bit rocky who was there trying to help me and steady me back onto my feet? Women. Whatever it was, a word of encouragement, a card, email, text, a hug, even a phone call, yes, some folks still use the phone, but at every turn it's been women building me back up. Actually you were one of those women as well."

Shay stood in front of me with this demeanor of are you done yet? But I continued.

"Whatever it was Shay it was to help us not lose hope and keep putting one foot in front of the other. It could have been as simple as them telling their own story to us, to let us know, we'll be fine as we endure our situation, too. They were helping to hold us up when we couldn't lift ourselves up at that particular time. Do you remember that time you were depressed and Jamala showed up at your door and made you get dressed?"

Jamala wasn't playing that day, she came in and said, "Get up, get dressed, you are not sitting in here another day, this pity party is over! Let's go! Get up, dust yourself off, we're out of here today!!!"

"I guess you don't remember that, and you're talking about you don't do women. Really? I can go on and on of how the ladies in our circle have run to one another's aid throughout the years, and you weren't excluded from that."

"Those ladies are in your circle, not mine."

"Okay Shay if that's what you want to say, but folks have been there for you too, even if it was on the strength of you being my cousin. So don't say you don't do women. Some have stayed up in the midnight hour listening to you before, just as they have with me."

"Whatever."

"And you know what else Shay?"

She sighed, but I continued, "You were also *that woman* on the other end always extending a hand and uplifting words to other women, well, that is, til' you changed."

I could see a piss off brewing on Shay as I continued reminding her of times women were there for her, she finally interrupted. "No one has helped me with anything."

"Really Shay, did you really fix your mouth to say that? Wow, so no one has helped you? Oh my God, how'd you fix your mouth to say that? If it wasn't your mother, it was your cousins, if it wasn't your cousins it was your aunts, your friends, what are you talking about you don't do women? You "did women" when you needed them. What does that mean you don't do women? Who makes a blanket statement like that, as if all women have done something to you?"

"Whatever."

"Truth be told we can be treated so badly by the opposite sex sometimes until we really need to try harder to step up how we treat one another because guess what? When the rubber meets the road, and one or two of the wheels fall off of this thing called life, it has always been women to step up for us. It's what we do."

"Speak for yourself. You do all this talk about women loving on each other and folks at your church can't even sit by one another. This clique always has to sit with this clique, what happened to loving on everyone at the church?"

"You always gotta take it back there don't you? Yeah we can do better there also."

"They can be so mean to one another right up in the church it makes outsiders like me wonder why we should go up in there, when we can get the same treatment in the street."

"Oh so this new Shay is an "outsider" when it comes to the church now? Okay. But you know what Shay, I'm going to agree with you on that one, you're right, but what I was saying is that you cannot deny the times of illness, bereavement, financial strain, relationship woes, divorce, whatever the case, it was the women in your life who huddled around to coach you on. It's what we do as women, we help one another through things because we've either just finished going through something or we know something else might be right around the corner coming our way and we'll need someone too."

"You can believe that if you want to Brooklyn, but like I said I don't do women. I don't like being around them, I don't trust them, I don't have any need for them, I don't like them. I wouldn't do you if you weren't my cousin."

"You might want to re-think that one Shay. You don't like other women, because you don't like yourself."

"Girl please. But, if you're sticking with these crazy birthday plans you have, I might have to miss this one, I ain't trying to sit up with a bunch of women. They're phony. They smile in your face and then turn their backs on you."

"Well I've heard it all."

"They are."

"You know what else I know to be true Shay, sometimes you don't like yourself so much that you can't like anyone."

"Well that's definitely not the case with me at all, so you can lose that idea right now. You must be talking about someone else with that one because I love myself. But, don't be surprised if you don't see me at your party honey because I don't do women."

"You know what else Shay, sometimes jealousy makes you not want to be around other women."

"Oh now you're talking crazy, there's not a woman alive that I'm jealous of, and definitely none of your friends."

"Yeah, this little party might have to go on without me."

She didn't know it, but that was music to my ears.

Shay started amusing herself by dancing and singing an oldie but goodie, *Smiling faces sometimes pretend to be your friend. Smiling faces show no traces of the evil that lurks within.*

She got all up in my face on the part that says, *Can you dig it?!*

With a bit more excitement than I thought I'd have I turned on my computer and started working on my Evite. My plans were to eat a little something first and then start working on the invitation, but found myself doing both at the same time, totally excited. I had a party to plan!!!

Three months prior, I'd reserved the large room at the Marina Casa restaurant, one of my absolute favorites. Again, I didn't have to think of a Plan B. The entrance to the restaurant was the first captivating view with much greenery and fish swimming in a pond. A short distance away boats swayed in the water. This was normally the first and last spot patrons stopped to take pictures. The rest of the restaurant, with its ocean view and decorative lights was just as breathtaking, but then again, I've always had this fascination with lights and water. It was a very tranquil ambience. I especially loved to be there when the sun sets, something I'd be able to experience again at my party. The food was excellent, they gave you a lot of it, and it was reasonably priced.

I always get a bit nervous whenever I plan something; panicking immediately, wondering what if no one shows up.

Gramby always said, "Honey folks will show up as long as there is food."

She was right, but that rule often changed when people were paying for their own meals.

I worked on the Evite until I was totally satisfied with it. I clicked on the button that allowed me to add some celebratory confetti to the online invitation. I knew some of the ladies wouldn't like my remark that I put at the bottom of the Evite, but I didn't care. It said, PLEASE ALLOW YOUR PRESENCE TO BE GIFT ENOUGH.

In other words, don't bring a gift, just come. Truly I felt paying for their own meals and spending the evening with me was more than I could ask for. It was gift enough. Time together...yes, for me that's what it was all about, seeing one another. Some I hadn't seen in many years, some I'd talked to but hadn't seen, others we hadn't talked or seen one another at all, some just mailed an annual Christmas card, so I was excited about fellowshipping together, catching up, laughing, it all sounded good to me.

I started scrolling through my phone contacts to add ladies to the Evite list. I smiled each time I got to a name and took a quick coast down memory lane about her. I got to Traci Bookman's name and laughed out loud thinking of her laugh, where she'd laugh so hard tears ran down her face, and before long everyone else was laughing. The only problem was none of us knew what Traci was laughing at in the first place, yet there we were hysterically laughing, too.

I got to Aubree's name and teared up a bit. It was her funeral service two years ago when we all said, "We need to stop meeting like this." I wished I could click her name to invite her, instead I pressed "delete" to finally remove her from the contact list.

Before long I had 48 ladies selected, which included Shay. I know a lot of kids don't listen to their mommas these days, but I still do, and she's the only reason I invited her.

Unlike U.S. Snail Mail the computer is instant, and so were some of the responses, and like a Nervous Nellie I had to look at each response as I heard my phone beep. I surely didn't know they were going to respond this quick, but how fun it was watching the responses come through.

"I'll be there, I wouldn't miss it."

"Girl, please don't tell me when I can and cannot bring a gift! See you soon Ladybug."

Wow, I haven't heard that one in a bit, Lady Bug; Dyanne has called me that for...wow I can't remember how many years.

"I wouldn't miss it, see you soon Brookie."

Brookie, lol, I haven't heard that in a while either.

"I'll be there...if the Lord says the same. Hahaha, I stole your line."

Thinking of two of my friends who refused to use technology, I created a quick invitation flyer for them to drop in the "snail mail."

I could hear Taylor's big mouth complaining about people who use computers to communicate all the time.

She'd always say, "Contact me the old fashioned way, you guys do know telephones still work don't you? All this mess has taken away the personal touch of communicating with one another and hearing each other's voices. What is it people can't talk anymore? I want to hear people's voices. Call me! Let my phone ring so I can answer it!! Hello!!!"

I laughed thinking of Taylor because she still carried a big hand written phone book in her purse, with a rubber band around it because it's so old and tattered, similar to the one Gramby used to have on her kitchen table when we were kids.

"Yeah, I'll still have all my numbers when your fancy phone crashes and you lose all your numbers. You can laugh at my phone book all you want."

For the sake of keeping the peace and making sure that Taylor and anyone else on snail mail didn't get offended that they weren't invited, I'd be going to the post office in the morning to mail their invitations.

My phone alerted me that I had another response, "Hey Brook, I won't be attending. I'll talk to you soon. Love you sis, Ashleigh."

I knew exactly what that was about, and I was already ahead of the game on this one. Ashleigh was having financial challenges and couldn't afford to come. But she'll see that's not a problem at all when she got home from work. I stopped by her house on my way home and dropped a gift card to the restaurant in her box to cover her expenses that night. I understood her situation, been there, done that, got the t-shirt. But, the night wouldn't be complete without her. As a matter of fact she was one of those friends I would have changed the date for her to attend if there was any conflict with her schedule, that's how much her presence meant to me. I wanted to give her something privately not to embarrass her, and not to put others in her business, so I thought sticking it in her mailbox would be the best way. Some people give what they have for someone in front of others, they want everyone to see it, to me that's self-glory. I guess it puffs them up, but as Gramby used to say, "That's their *only* reward, the self-gratification of doing things in front of others so everyone else sees what you did, but in reality God's the only one who needs to see it and get the glory."

It was very easy to drop the gift card in Ashleigh's mailbox, because I could recall times when someone dropped something in mine, too.

Let he/she who is without sin cast the first stone.

Every time you subtract negative from your life, you make room for more positive.

Life truly is a journey, and the less baggage we carry the easier the ride.

Do Not Judge: You don't know what storm I've asked them to go through, and what testimony I'm trying to give them. God

Good friends are hard to find, harder to leave, and impossible to forget.

Best friends are the people you can do anything, or nothing with and still have the best time.

Remember you don't need a certain number of friends, just a number of friends you can be certain of.

CHAPTER

Three

Each time I stirred during the night I picked up my phone to check if any more RSVP's came in. One thing I was now certain of was that I would not be at the restaurant celebrating alone. So far 25 RSVP's, and I was as excited as a kid in a candy store.

I set up the Evite to where everyone could see who was invited and see their responses and comments. I thought that would be nice for others to see who was coming and get just as excited as I was in anticipation of seeing one another.

My phone rang, "Hello."

Shay, "Hey, I got your invitation, Evite or whatever they call them."

"Oh, okay. What's up?"

I was thinking Shay was possibly calling to tell me of some typo on the Evite, or that perhaps I got the date wrong or something. Maybe I looked at the calendar wrong and the numerical date wasn't adding up with the Saturday I chose. Or better yet, maybe she was calling to say she wouldn't be attending.

"Are you crazy?"

Deep breath. "Am I crazy about what Shay?"

"I see you invited Trisha."

"Yeah, and...(before I could complete my sentence she interrupted)

"Girl, who invites their ex-husband's wife to their birthday party, that's crazy? Who does that?"

"Me. I do that Shay; you see her name on the list don't you? Well, I invited her."

"You can't be serious. Why did you invite her?"

"Because we're friends, and I want her to come, what other reason do you invite people to your birthday party?"

"Girl please. Did you forget that's your ex-husband's new wife?"

"Yeah, I know who she is Shay. I also know I'm not going to keep going through this every time you see someone on my list that you don't like. I don't have to dislike everyone you don't like. And by the way, I get along fine with Trisha, and if you can remember she's the one who worked with me with my school schedule and the kids to finish my degree a few years ago. I couldn't have done it without her, and by the way, she treats my kids as though they are her own."

"Yeah, that's the point. She acts like she's their mother."

"No she doesn't. All I know is Trisha was probably the most mature of the three of us at one point. She's the one who helped make this blended family thing work so well."

"Ain't no way in the world I'd invite her and act like she's my friend."

"That's you Shay. She's never done anything to me, not one thing."

"That's crazy to me."

"I see you're inviting Jourdain too."

"What is it Shay, are you going to go down the whole list of people and tell me who I invited? Guess what?"

"What?"

"I made the list, so I already know who I invited."

Shay reminded me of those crazy folks on Facebook who snoop and never post or comment on anything, but will call you and tell you what you posted. "Oh you were at the Cheesecake Factory."

I know I was at the Cheesecake Factory; I'm the one who posted it! Now here was Shay calling to critique everyone on my invite list.

Shay, "I can't for the life of me see why you would invite her when she didn't do right by you that time. No, seriously, did you forget Jourdain never paid you back that money she owed you?"

"No I didn't forget Shay. But did you forget that's been over 25 years ago now? How long am I supposed to be mad over that? It's a lesson learned Shay."

"Well she was wrong."

"I never said she wasn't wrong; but to answer your question, yes I invited her and I hope she comes. This is what I'm talking about; you always have an issue with something. This isn't your birthday gathering, and anyone on my invitation list shouldn't be your issue."

"That's crazy."

"It's crazy to you Shay because you hold on to everything, you stay mad at people so long you forget what you were mad at in the first place. You're still mad at that girl who said something to you in high school, really Shay? Who stays mad that long, and do you even remember what she said? I bet you're the only one who still thinks about it, because often others have totally forgotten about stuff and gone on their merry way, but you continue to carry it. No seriously, we are almost 50, who stays mad at something since high school?"

I laughed a bit, and that seemed to rub Shay the wrong way.

She just about bit my head off, "So it's funny to you huh?"

"Yeah it is funny that someone can stay mad for all those years, yet can't remember what they're mad at. Tell me what did she say to you Shay? Come on tell me, in eleventh grade what did she say to you that you're still mad today? You can't remember huh?"

"Whatever Brooklyn."

I can't lie I went a period of being ticked off at Jourdain, but I call it a lesson learned. Gramby used to always tell us, "Don't loan money to people because they get amnesia, you don't want to give any of your friends amnesia do you?" That lady would crack her own self up with the things she said.

"Have you noticed every time you loan a friend money they forget to pay you?"

"Yes, Gramby."

"I mean they plumb forget they owed you money, but that will learn you, not to loan out money you can't afford to give out in the first place. And not only do they forget, they somehow are the ones who get mad at you and start avoiding you."

That was so true. Quite amazing how the person in the wrong winds up with the attitude, how does someone get mad because you ask for your money back I'll never understand? But, I'm well over that. Jourdain was in my life so long until I feel this night wouldn't be the same without her either. Sure I had days where that three hundred was needed, but I certainly never missed a meal, never once had any utilities turned off, late car note, house note, or anything, and I learned a lesson. And contrary to how Shay feels about things, I'm glad she's coming.

"Look Shay, I've got to go. I have some things I absolutely have to finish for tomorrow. I have couples coming in early."

Again, a time when Shay could have kept her mouth shut, she said, "It's funny how you're a marriage counselor and couldn't keep your own marriage together."

Deep breath. "Bye Shay."

"Oh I guess I said something wrong."

"You say a lot of things most people wouldn't say, and would feel weren't necessary to say in the first place. Good night Shay."

"I just think it's something that you counsel people on keeping their marriages together but you wound up in divorce court. I'm not sure I'd want a marriage counselor counseling me who didn't succeed at their own."

"Bye Shay."

"Wait, let's go shopping before your birthday dinner and get you an outfit."

"I don't need an outfit Shay."

"I don't get why you don't treat yourself more often, you only live once."

"I treat myself enough, and I'd like to know what money tree you shook and have so much money to spend all the time."

"I work."

"Yeah, okay, me too."

"No seriously let's go out and get us something to wear to the dinner. I'll buy it."

"I'm good; I don't need you to buy it Shay, I have money. I'll find something in my closet."

"You haven't seen these women in years and it's your party."

"Exactly, so they won't know if it's new or not, right?"

"You need something new for your birthday, I'll buy it."

"Like I said Shay, I can buy it myself if I wanted it, but I don't need it. You seem to be rolling in dough, one of those sugar daddies giving you money?"

"Just one Sugar Daddy, not "daddies," and I don't care a thing about him; I'm with him to spend his money that's it, that's all, and when the money runs out, I'm running out, too. I'm now that woman who treats men as low down as they've treated me. Like them, I don't care either. If anyone gets hurt in relationships now it won't be me I can tell you that now."

"Wow, so because you've been hurt a few times, you're going to mistreat anyone else who comes your way? How's that right?"

"It's right to me, and that's all that matters. You live by that *do unto others as you would have them do unto you* rule. I live by the *get them before they get me again* rule."

"Wow Shay. You know that type of stuff comes back to you."

"Girl please, don't start with that one. Everyone who has dogged me seems to be doing mighty fine, as a matter of fact they seem to be doing better than ever, ain't a thing came back to them, so all that what goes around comes around stuff is not true. Look at Blake, my good ol' first husband, he left me to go live under a roof with someone else where he raised her kids, leaving his own kids in a household without a father. And, yeah I'm still pissed."

"You ever thought the attitude pushed him away?"

"What?"

I knew this conversation would go way out in left field from this point so I said, "You know what girl, I need to go and get some things done for work tomorrow. It's late. And we have something at church tomorrow night as well."

"Okay, I'll talk to you later; I was just shocked at some of the folks on this Evite list. Hey maybe I'll come go to church with you tomorrow. I need to see that handsome Pastor of yours anyway."

"Don't start Shay."

"Don't start what?"

"You know. You know he's married."

"Yeah, yeah, he was married when this current wife was sleeping with him too wasn't he?"

"And you wonder why no one wants to be around you. It's your mouth Shay."

"Well it's the truth. I'm sure I can get his attention. He's a man."

"What do you mean by that?"

"He's a man like all the rest."

"All men aren't the same Shay. Look, I've got to go. I'm hanging up. I'm not going through this with you again. I'm done. I've got stuff to do. Bye."

"Wait, wait, why'd you invite Shelby? She stopped calling you and everything; she wouldn't even return your calls."

"I invited her because I want to see her Shay, is that a good enough reason? I want to see her! What other answer do you need? Do you know how many times I've held out not calling someone because I had that they can call me just as well as I can call them attitude, only to find out they were sick, or going through something where they actually needed a friend, which was the case with Shelby. Now, I don't worry about who calls me and who doesn't call me anymore Shay. I just pick up the doggone phone and call them myself. Life is way too short. And how is it hurting me to pick up the phone, I'm not losing one thing by making that move to call them. If you remember it was too late when I finally dialed Joi's number. All that time I held out not calling her because she never called me, and the girl was sick and then died. I felt so bad after that. I'm not playing that game anymore. If they cross my mind, I'm calling, regardless to whether they've called me or returned my last call."

"Oh there you go with all that. It's always a sermon huh Brooklyn? So people can treat you any type of way and it's okay."

"I didn't say that Shay, but Shelby not returning my call doesn't mean I can't call her. I don't get mad at everything like you do. I'm glad I called her, she was sick and I was able to go by there and do some things for her. I'd like to think I lifted her spirits. I'd like to think if I was sick someone would do the same for me. But anyway, I'm hanging up; anyone who has a problem with someone on my list needs to stay home. For real I've got to go. Bye.

After getting off the phone with Shay, and organizing myself for another busy Monday, I checked my Fitbit status and thought how ridiculous this was to be running in place in my room before bathing, to outscore the top stepper of the day. I'm gonna win this challenge today!!!

When someone judges you, it isn't actually about you, it's about them; their own insecurities, limitations, and needs.

It's funny how people judge other people's mistakes while they also do the same thing.

Don't judge my past, I don't live there anymore.

If one day you're feeling like crying, call me. I can't promise to make you laugh, but I'm willing to cry with you.

In the end, we will remember not the words of our enemies, but the silence of our friends.

CHAPTER

Four

"Brooklyn party!"

"My goodness, this must be my lucky day," the waiter said as he prepared to lead us to our table.

"What's the occasion? Birthday? Baby shower?"

Evette responded, "Are you crazy, you've been over at that bar too long, do any of us look as though we would be, or better yet, should be having a baby or a baby shower?"

We all laughed at the waiter's expression. Everyone seemed to be in light spirits.

Cyn, who attended school with me dating back to pre-school said, "Girl I needed this break. I call this my commercial break from my real life. I'm not thinking of anything and anyone outside of this restaurant tonight. I am so glad to be out I don't know what to do. The nurse said she would stay a few extra hours with my mother and for me to go out and enjoy myself, and that's exactly what I plan to do. Somehow out of six kids I'm the only one there taking care of my mother and that Alzheimer's ain't no joke. Sometimes I do wonder why others haven't or don't pitch in since it's their mother too, but instead of posing that question to them I ask the Lord for strength to make it through another day. I don't worry about tomorrow's strength, I just ask Him to get me through *this day*. My sister has the nerves to always comment on how Mom doesn't even know who we are anymore. I'm still trying to figure out what she's thinking when she says that because the way I see it, it doesn't matter if she remembers us or not, she still needs to be cared for, and she's still our mother. How about we remember all she's done for us throughout our lives and not worry about what this mean disease has done to her, causing her not to remember her own children? Yeah, how about that? I don't care what anyone says, sometimes the caregiver needs some care too, and that's why I'm so glad to be out tonight. I needed this break."

"I hear you Cyn. I hear you loud and clear, I needed to get out, too. I've been taking care of my father the last few years, and it's hard. There's no other way to describe it, it's hard. But I'm sure you feel the same, no matter how hard it is, you'd do it for as long as you have to."

"You got that right Val."

Sandy chimed in, "I'm taking care of my husband's mother now. Life is funny, my husband complained about how he wasn't getting attention when I was taking care of my own mother, complaining that I was never at home, that I wasn't spending enough time with him, but oh, when his mother got sick he didn't say a word, not one complaint about how much I was gone taking care of her, and how I don't cook anymore, and how I'm at the hospital all the time. Nothing. But, believe me; I'm taking care of his mother just as well as I took care of my own. You ladies are right, the caregiver needs some care sometimes too, and I'm glad to be out tonight."

"I get so stuck in this routine until I hardly do anything I consider fun. Same thing, same time, same everything, nothing different."

"Yeah, that's me too T, it turns out to be work and home, work and home, nothing exciting, just the same thing, all work and no play."

Toni walked into the restaurant, and as usual she had photo albums of her kids.

"Please tell me that girl doesn't have all those photo albums with her again, somebody please tell her this is an adult affair and we are not trying to look at kids tonight. I don't want to see mine, and I sure don't want to see hers."

Toni whacked Toyia upside the head with one of the smaller albums.

"Girl put those photo albums up; we see all fifty of the pictures you post on Facebook *daily*. We've probably already seen those. You don't let them grow an inch before posting more on Facebook every day."

We all laughed, including Toni. Everyone knew and loved Toyia's personality, because truly some folk's feelings would have been hurt if someone else had said that to them, but Toyia had a way of saying things that we all felt like saying, but the comedian in her allowed it to go over well.

Toni, "Okay, so you guys don't want to see my babies."

Toni slid her photo albums inside the decorative bag she carried them in. We all knew those pictures wouldn't be in the bag long. She'd find someone to show them to.

The waiter, "Ladies, please follow me. Well what's the occasion?"

"It's a Girls in My Circle Night."

"Oh this is some type of club getting together."

"No. It's a Girls in My Circle Night."

The waiter looked perplexed. "It's my birthday and these are all of the girls in my circle, some of us go all the way back to pre-school and first grade."

"Ohhh, that's pretty cool. I would have to rent some friends to have this many people show up for my birthday. I'd have to go on social media or something and invite strangers and hope they showed up, or pay some folks to come. Shoot, to tell you the truth the few friends I do have would probably only come if it was free."

"Stop it. You're kidding, right? I'm sure your friends would come and you wouldn't have to rent any friends."

"No seriously, I would." He laughed.

"Well, let me tell you, you don't have a clue how long I've been trying to have all these old friends together."

"You must be mistaking because I don't see anyone old here."

"Oh my dear, we're going to get along just fine." (Laughter)

"Well looks like you finally succeeded, and again, this must be my lucky day to serve all of you beautiful young ladies, if we can continue down this way to the reserved room, we will get you seated."

He looked over at the other waiter patiently waiting to assist him and said, "Fifty shades of brown."

I asked, "What did you say?"

With a nervous giggle, "Nothing ma'am."

"Yes you did, I heard you say something, but you stand corrected, it's about 45 shades of brown, not quite 50. I told you I heard you. You didn't think I could hear that well, huh?"

All the ladies laughed while some patrons looked over as if to say *I sure hope they don't sit by us with all that noise.* But we all kept pressing pass them to the enclosed glassed room in the back of the restaurant, all the while steadily having conversations, steadily moving and talking, so excited to catch up on things we couldn't wait to get to the reserved room to start chatting.

Stella was still holding the vibrating pager that alerts patrons when it's time to be seated. Being her usual crazy self, she turned to the waiter who had his hand extended to retrieve the pager from her, and said, "Can I take this home?"

Some of us laughed knowing what she was alluding to, and others disgustedly said, "Stella!!!" Something we were used to saying when it came to Stella anyway, nothing new. The older that girl got the crazier she was.

Carrie, "Girl, give that man back that thing?"

Stella, laughing of course, "Girl please, you need to be asking him for another one, because I think you're in the same boat I'm in."

The whole conversation seemed to go over the young waiter's head.

It sounded as though a hundred different conversations were going as everyone made their way to and into the dining room. Once there I noticed everyone entered the door, but stood hovering at the entrance.

I asked, "What are you guys waiting for?"

"Oh we didn't know if it was assigned seating, or if you were saving seats for anyone?"

I replied, "Ladies please, there is none of that up in here tonight. Please sit wherever you'd like."

The way I saw it each lady was just as important as the next, and I wanted them to feel as such. One thing that has always annoyed me was the way a clique of women has to sit together all the time, as though sitting with someone else, and meeting other females is beyond them. I recall one 50th birthday party I went to where a lady from church put an article of clothing, an accessory or something in each chair at the table to reserve for her usual group, because God forbid you have to sit with an "outsider."

I've also been to events where ladies arrived late and squeezed their big butts at a table where there was clearly no room to sit in the first place, all because they absolutely have to sit with their normal clique. Sure, other tables were available where everyone could be comfortably seated, but again, God forbid you have to sit with someone different.

The ladies maneuvered around to their seats, still chatting and trying to get quick updates on one another.

"Brooklyn, so where are you sitting?"

"Don't worry about me; I just need to know y'all are alright?"

"I'll get in where I fit in."

Toyia turned to the waiters, "This girl is talking about she'll get in where she fits in, and it's her birthday, let's put her in the middle here. Can you bring those flowers down here in the center? We'll put the birthday girl in the middle here."

The waiters patiently waited for everyone to put their gifts on the table, and take their seats. They then introduced themselves. "Wow this is a large party. I'm Pierre, this is Te'ray, Nesha, and Sabrina, and we're here to serve you tonight. We will go and get water and come get your drink orders. If you need us, just wave your hand."

Shante waved her hand, "Let me make it easy on you, how about bringing some pitchers of mango margaritas and we should be good for a minute."

"That's Shante."

"Well, I'm just trying to make it easy on them."

"Will do. How many am I bringing?"

Shante responded, "Enough to cover everyone who'd like to partake, don't worry, I'll cover that order."

"Okay, we will bring some water and those pitchers out for you, and get other drink orders as well when we return."

I listened to all the conversations. I heard Gayla say, "No you're not still in the city; I thought you had moved away."

That was the sad part about it, most of us were all still in the general area we were when we grew up, maybe one or two had moved thirty minutes to an hour out, but yes we were all still right in the local neighborhoods and hadn't seen one another.

"How's your mother? Is she still over on Lake Avenue? You still married? How are the kids?"

Folks were spewing out questions so fast others had to play catch up to answer them all.

Yes, Mom is still in the same place. My dad is still around too. He lives on the same street."

"Same street?"

"Yeah, some folks are fine living in separate bedrooms, same house, but they seem to get along better in different houses, same street."

"Whew, I've heard it all. Now that's funny!"

"Yes, I'm still married."

"Girl that's awesome, you must be going on about 30 years of marriage now. How'd you manage that?"

"Kept folks out of our business."

"Ain't that the truth."

"Well these days marriages don't make it 30 days, so truly congratulations are in order for 30 years!"

"Whatever happened to Jamille, where's she?"

"She's probably somewhere in somebody's business. I had to get her out of my business. It's amazing how the women who don't have a man can always tell you what you should do with yours. So we're not nearly as close as we used to be."

I caught bits and pieces of many of the different conversations, sometimes able to ascertain whose voice was speaking, and sometimes not. The room was loud with chatter and laughter.

"Brooklyn this is so nice, what made you plan this?"

"Well it's the only thing I could think of that I really wanted to do for my birthday."

"Ahhhh, isn't she sweet."

I gave Elyse one of those, "shut up girl" looks as her tone seemed to be teasing me.

"No seriously, I get so tired of the same ol' thing of us all running into one another at different places: the doctor's office, grocery store, mall, etc., usually at a funeral, and saying the same ol' thing."

"What same ol' thing?"

"Oh you know how we always say, we need to quit meeting like this, and we need to get together more often, but never make it happen?"

"Oh okay."

"Then the next funeral or event we say the same thing again. We even add a little bit more to it sometimes."

"Like what?"

"Oh you know how we say, you know tomorrow isn't promised we need to do better at getting together. We need to make a conscious effort to make this happen, no excuses."

"Yeah, that is so true; I've said that a lot of times myself, I just told someone that very thing last week."

"I swear I just told someone that two months ago, and the bad thing about it is I said I would be the one planning something within the month and never did. Life happens and you don't get around to doing things like this."

I continued, "Anyway, I wanted ladies who were special to me to all be together without a casket propped up in front of us. I didn't want anyone saying they didn't want to come because they didn't have a date, so I made it all about us ladies. But I'm so glad we're not at a church with the organ playing and dabbing our eyes because another friend passed away. Shoot, I'm just glad to see you all."

"Okay, okay, enough of this." Pat said as she reached for her napkin. I was glad Krista shifted the conversation.

"Did you see on the invitation where she said NO GIFTS PLEASE, YOUR PRESENCE IS GIFT ENOUGH? How is she going to tell someone not to bring a gift?"

"Well you know that's Brooklyn. She'll empty her pockets doing stuff for other people, but will tell you not to do something for her."

"What I want to know is when have we *ever* listened to Brooklyn?"

Someone on the end of the table hollered, "Never!!!"

Everyone busted up!

I started off planning this to where I would take the entire bill, but then I came to my senses when house taxes came around for both my properties. I felt since everyone was paying for their own food that I would let them know that that was gift enough, but obviously that didn't go over very well by the looks of all the gifts on the table.

"Girl please, the day I have a birthday party and ask people not to bring gifts will be the day when I… when I…when I…shoot I can't even think of a time that would happen."

"High five me on that one Bo, I'm with you girl, bring the gifts! Bring the gifts!"

Some of the ladies commented on Renette's size, it seemed she was still the same tiny she was in junior high school, but could eat any and everything in sight.

"What size are you now? It doesn't look like you've changed a bit, and you've had three kids?"

"An 8."

"An 8? Girl please I haven't been an 8 since I was 8 years old."

A loud roar of laughter filled the room, so loud other patrons looked towards our private dining area.

"Brook, this restaurant is beautiful. It always has been, but the upgrades they made are gorgeous."

It felt good to get some positive feedback from people. It did my heart good to see they all thought this was such a great idea, and well needed event. I'd heard so much negative from Shay regarding my birthday plans until something positive was rather uplifting and quite refreshing. All of my anxiety and nervousness of how my birthday plans would be received, and how my event would turn out quickly vanished.

"I've always loved this place Brooklyn, the food is really good, and you get a lot of it."

I finally looked up and noticed that everyone had some shade of lavender on, even my dress was lavender and black.

"Wait a minute, what's with all this lavender?"

"Oh we saw the invitation was lavender so we thought that's what you wanted us to wear."

"Oh for real, is that how you tell the color scheme of an event, I swear I never knew that. I just picked a color for the Evite. Well I guess you learn something every day."

"Brooklyn you didn't know that?"

"Like I said, I guess you learn something new every day."

"Duh."

Everyone laughed.

We laughed for more reasons than one. It was so good to see one another. By the time the waiters returned with the water, some of us were already tearing up and dabbing our eyes from laughter. And, of course, some of the "remember when" stories caused a few tears to fall for other reasons as well.

Cheryl's name came up and we thought of how positive she was all the time. Through some of her hardest times and even our own hard times, she always said, "Man we're going to have some testimony when we get through this mess. Shoot, we might have to have a Testimony Sharing Party."

The last time I visited Cheryl in the hospital I looked all over the place for her. And, you know it's really, really not funny to get to a hospital to visit someone and they're nowhere to be found, and the bed is made up. I felt my stomach drop when I turned into her room and she was not there. Finally a lady visiting someone else in the same room said, "Oh she was just here, a visitor came to see her and they went for a walk."

I went up and down this hallway and down another, I went to another floor's waiting area as directed by a security guard to look for her there, I was everywhere. I finally left the hospital headed home, and who did I see sitting under a tree? Cheryl.

"Girl what are you doing out here, I've been looking all over for you?"

Cheryl said, "Taking in God's glory, it's beautiful out here, no need of me being cooped up in a hospital if I can make my way outside, right?"

Different ladies started reminiscing about Cheryl.

"Yeah, that's Cheryl; she'd always been that way. She flipped it to the positive every chance she got."

"All I can remember is her sending me scriptures to encourage my sister through her breast cancer situation; there she was on her deathbed herself but still thinking of others."

"How'd that just happen? Would be the question I asked myself every single time I got on the elevator after my visit with Cheryl. I swear I would say *okay, so you came here to encourage her, and she flipped it on you and encouraged you again.*"

"Yeah, I felt the same way every time I saw her, too."

A few more stories went around about Cheryl and her love for music and dj'ing and after we dabbed a few eyes someone said, "Okay, that's enough let's change the subject."

"I can hear Cheryl now, y'all stop all that crying, wetting up all those napkins, stop it!"

"Yeah, then she'd sing some words to a song."

"Yeah, probably now she'd sing I Hope You Dance. *May you never take one single breath for granted. Dance!*

"Man I miss that girl."

Of course it took no time for the twins Meghan and Regan to chime in on how I could never tell them apart, and quite honestly I still couldn't. Meghan had some type of mole under her chin, and each time I was in their presence I lifted their chins to figure out who I was talking to. Some said they told them apart by their different personalities, but quite honestly I didn't see a difference there either. But of course they had to tell their "remember when" story.

"Remember when Brooklyn wanted to get Regan back for something she'd done and was planning some prank, and she thought she was talking to Meghan, but was actually talking to Regan."

"Whew that was funny."

The remember when stories continued and continued, but of course the one that cracked everyone up was the one Evette told so well. Kay rolled her eyes, assuming Evette was about to tell a story about her, and she assumed right.

"Okay, okay, wait…let me get myself together." Evette couldn't tell the story for laughing so hard.

"Okay, okay, here I go, I'm gonna tell it this time for real."

"Look at her; she's laughing so hard she can't get the story out."

"Okay, let me stop laughing."

By now others were already laughing just because Evette was laughing.

"Okay, who remembers that time we were all going to get in shape and we started going to this exercise class?"

"Oh Lord," Kay said, wishing she didn't have to hear this story again.

Okay, okay, let me stop laughing first. I'm sorry, but this was funny. So, we get there and we're signing in on the sign in sheet, and speaking to other ladies present. One of the younger ladies there was Kay's goddaughter, Jasmine. Jazz had on a gray shirt, and black capris. She wore long braids, but to exercise she had pinned her hair up. Well, it's time to get started. The instructor got us started with some stretching; two seconds into the stretch Kay decided to reach her hand forward and pinch Jasmine on the butt. Only one problem."

"What?"

"It wasn't Jasmine?"

"Huh?"

"Another lady turned around and said, "What's going on here?""

"You should have seen Kay's face when this lady turned around. It wasn't Jasmine, it was a lady with a gray shirt and black capris and braids just like Jasmine, but it wasn't Jasmine."

"Oh my God, really?"

The entire room exploded with laughter.

"Whew, I'm sorry, that's still funny to me."

Kay, rolling her eyes, said, "I'm so sick of her telling that same story; don't you have another story to tell?"

Evette cracked up, "Yeah I have some others to tell, but I don't have any as funny as that one. All I know is that was funny. Whew, you can't make this stuff up. And she didn't take a little bitty pinch of this stranger's butt; I mean she grabbed a handful."

Kay smirked, and told Evette, "It's not that funny!"

But, others along with Evette in unison all said, "YES IT IS!!!!"

The waiters brought the pitchers of mango margaritas and took a few other orders, and the room was still roaring with laughter.

As I listened to all the laughter in the room, I thought about the scripture that speaks of a merry heart being like medicine. I figured all this laughter must've done much healing this night for sure. I laughed so hard my stomach hurt. It was funny watching ladies hardly able to contain themselves as they impatiently waited their turn to jump into all the different conversations on this walk down memory lane. It was fun watching it all unfold, everyone anxiously waiting to add their two cents.

I couldn't keep up with all of the conversations, but I knew it was Evette's crazy self when I heard, "Girl when you get this age you can't just assume it's gas anymore."

"Girl you are too funny, but you're telling the truth."

Evette continued, "And have you noticed all of our problems start with men?"

"What?"

"Yeah, all of our problems start with men, MENopause, MENstrual cramps, MENtal breakdown."

"Evette stop, this girl is still a mess."

"Evette, we're going to have to put you out of here. Oh my goodness, I can't remember the last time I laughed this hard."

My ears were trying to capture as many of the conversations as I could. I heard Marla, the doctor in the group, doing what she always does.

Marla, "It's so important that we get our mammograms, early detection save lives. You know my slogan: *No lumps in my cups.*

Another conversation was brewing down on the other end, and I missed it from lingering laughter from Evette's craziness, but I heard Julie say, "Now she knows that is not how the story went, she's lying on me. Oooh Tasha you know you twisted that story. That was not me, that was you and you know it!!!"

"Tasha never could tell a story right. Remember how we'd play that game where you started off telling a story, and each person told the story privately to the person next to them, until it made its way around the entire table to the person who told the original story to the first person? Well guess where the story would always change and wouldn't be close to the original story?"

Several ladies hollered out, "WITH TASHA!!!"

Tasha, "You guys are so wrong. That is not true."

As I watched everyone interacting I was ever so grateful that Plan A was the only plan I needed for my birthday.

"Brook thanks so much for planning this, honestly we get so caught up with life until we don't do things like this anymore, and we need it. You look up and wonder where the years went. I really needed this. I know this is your birthday, but it's so much like you to do something that we all needed. We need to pause sometimes. I'll speak for myself here girl, I am so happy to see all of you lovely ladies. Thanks Brook."

"You're welcome."

"I agree, thank you so much. We've all been through things, and praise God we don't look like what we've gone through."

Shelby waved her hands in the air, "Praise God I don't look like what I've been through, you guys wouldn't have recognized me if I did. Whew, thank you Lord."

Shelby dabbed her eyes, no doubt taking a quick glance over her life and the health issues she has faced.

Chimene spoke, "And please let me say this, Blare you haven't been in contact with anyone for a long time, I get that, and I'm not trying to put you on the spot, but it's good to see you girl. We love you. Okay, so your son did something that embarrassed you. It happens. Get up!! We try to raise them the best we can, but there are a lot of teachers out there, and sometimes they choose the wrong ones to follow, but don't ever think you have to stay away from your sisters. No one ever judged you. We've got you!! Believe me, we've all been through a myriad of things, from divorce, to standing in jail lines ourselves, illnesses, raising grandkids because our own kids are out there doing whatever, but we've got to keep going through until the sun starts shining again, one day at a time. Just because some of us don't talk about what we're going through, doesn't mean we aren't or haven't gone through something. Believe me we've all been through something, or, just came out of something, or about to go through something, but don't get embarrassed and stay away, let's lean on one another, pray for one another, and remember folks don't have to know every single detail of your situation to pray. Oh, we may not talk or see one another all the time, but watch us spring into action when one of us needs something, girl let that rubber meet the road and we're there. There are so many stories at this table, and sometimes we thought stuff would take us out of here, but we're still standing. Just pray for the strength to get through… one day at a time."

"Did she say one day at a time?"

"Girl it's been so tough sometimes I couldn't concentrate on one day at a time, I had to take it down to one minute at a time…just get me through this next minute."

"Whew, I hear you."

Blare teared up at Chimene's words, so Evette chimed in with, "Hey, you know what they say; women are like tea bags, they don't know how strong they are until they are in hot water. Again I say, thank God we don't look like what we've been through."

Amens filled the room,

Evette held up her glass, "I'll toast to that."

I took it all in, ladies who once held grudges had forgotten about all the stuff that didn't matter in the first place. They'd learned to not sweat the small stuff. They'd learned to let go of the baggage. Ladies who didn't really care for one another long ago were all hugged up laughing, exchanging numbers, taking selfies and seemed as though they were the "bestest" friends and seemed to have realized they had no reason at all for not liking that person then, or now. It seemed we'd all been given a good dose of "grow up," and were now mature and embracing one another.

I thought about how in my own adult life, and in recent years I might add, when a young lady approached me and informed me that when she first started seeing me at church she didn't like me. Yes, she'd never met me, didn't know a thing about me, but she didn't like me. Oh, I wasn't shocked that someone wouldn't like me, because everyone isn't going to like you, but what I was surprised about was that she took the time to tell me. I just feel that's a bit of information one generally keeps to them self. But she didn't keep me hanging; you know sometimes you don't have a clue why someone doesn't like you. But, she told me.

"I saw a *peace* in you that I didn't have in my own life at the time, and you irritated me. Yes, that's pretty sad, I know, but, it's the truth. You carry yourself with such confidence, and you always seemed so happy and at peace, and my life was so torn up at the time I was jealous of the peace you had, you acted as though everything was perfect in your life, as though you didn't have a care in the world."

She was right; I *acted* like everything was fine. It wasn't, I just carried my load differently than her.

Surely we women can be pretty tough on one another sometimes, *for no reason*. We just choose not to like someone.

But, I know firsthand what it feels like to have someone dislike you for no reason at all. What I also know even more than that is a friendship can be formed in spite of it all. Today, this young lady and I love one another to death. Oh I have my days where I get my digs in and tease her by asking her, "Do you like me today, or should I come back another day when you like me?"

We laugh, but sometimes you have to flip that negative into a positive, and that appears to be exactly what many of the Girls In My Circle have done.

The jazz that had been playing in the room stopped, and the theme song of Golden Girls started. The ladies laughed.

"No she didn't. She used to love that show when we were in school."

"Do you remember when Brooklyn would bounce around singing that in the hallways? That girl would get right up in your face as loud as she could sing."

"And didn't care who was around either."

"Oh there she goes again with that catsup bottle, that girl hasn't changed a bit."

I started singing into the mic (well the catsup bottle) as I did when we were younger. I hit the chorus, *Thank you for being a friend.*

"Look at her; she's still crazy as a Betsy bug."

I continued singing with everything I had, *and if you threw a party, invited everyone you knew…*

Before long other ladies chimed in with me, *thank you for being a friend.*

I heard an outburst of laughter, it was at that time I turned and saw the slide show had begun. There all the pictures I selected of myself were scrolling and fading across the big screen. Some ladies pointed and laughed, others said, "Oh I remember that one."

"I have that picture."

I looked at the pictures and had to laugh at a few myself. The plaid skirt set was an outfit I wore where no one could tell me I wasn't dressed up, but boy was it funny to look at now.

"No, she was in my class that year; we were about nine years old then."

"Instead of telling us not to bring gifts, you should have told us to bring some Depends, cause I'm about to pee on myself. Whew, look at that picture there with no teeth, that girl was snag-a-tooth."

"Yeah buddy, the tooth fairy had to pay a lot of money that month."

"You guys aren't right, but I'll get you back."

No one knew what I was talking about at that moment, but just as sure as they were all cracking up laughing at me, I'd get my laugh in too.

For some reason I slipped off a second, and was jolted from those thoughts when Sasha said, "Earth to Brooklyn."

"You okay?"

"Yes, I slipped off a minute. Reflecting. I'm grateful, that's all."

Feeling a little mushy I whispered, "I'm grateful, I'm just checking all my girls out, just taking it all in."

Actually my mind slipped off somewhere without notice, for each lady the waiter sat an appetizer plate in front of I looked at her and took a quick trip down memory lane. I thought of something that stuck with me about that particular lady. I then thought of all the testimonies of strength represented at the table as I looked at each lady. We'd all been through some knee buckling experiences in life, and now stood so tall. Thank you Lord for that. A tear fell, and though I thought it went unnoticed it didn't and different ladies started asking me what was wrong.

"I'm fine, nothing is wrong, I took a quick trip down memory lane, but I'm back now."

"Well take us with you next time."

I dabbed my eyes with the napkin, as the waiters came with more non-alcoholic beverage orders.

Evette, "Oh I'm sorry Sharron; I offered you a margarita and forgot you don't drink."

"Oh don't mind me, I've been clean 25 years now, and ain't nothing anyone could do to make me break that cycle. I lost everything once, and that was enough for me. Remember you guys were the light weights, one margarita and you guys were done, I'm the one who didn't know my limits, but I'm good now."

"That's awesome. What a blessing!"

The waiter came by and asked if he could pour me another margarita, "No thank you, I'm good, but if I didn't know any better I'd think you were flirting with me."

He laughed.

Bree raised her glass, "I'd like to make a toast to the birthday girl and for all these years of sisterhood-friendship represented here tonight. Brooklyn, thanks for being the common denominator, the one who links us all together. Thanks for allowing us to share your birthday with you, we needed this, and it took someone special like you to make it happen. Thanks for all the secrets you've kept throughout the years, and the effort you've made to keep in touch with as many of us as possible throughout the years, and wanting to share your 50th with all of us crazy women. We love you! Cheers!"

"Cheers!"

The pictures on the video screen still scrolled, but the thumb drive had been changed to include different pictures. This one included pictures of me and everyone else in the room throughout the years. I'd even stolen some off of Facebook. So now I could laugh too.

Before anyone noticed the same pictures were no longer scrolling, six huge trays of appetizers were delivered full of wings, sliders, potato skins, egg rolls, veggies, guacamole and more.

I turned to one of the waiters, "We didn't give an appetizer order yet."

"Oh, don't worry about it, we were told these were ordered for the Brooklyn party, this is the Brooklyn party right?"

"Well yes, but I made all the reservations and plans for this night and I sure didn't order all these appetizer trays."

We all looked perplexed. I turned to the waiter again, "Where'd these come from? We didn't order these."

The head waiter, Pierre, looking as lost as the rest of us responded, "I don't know ma'am, we were told they were for this party and so here they are, so dig in. Enjoy ladies. I'm leaving them here per the manager."

Evette, "Shoot, they don't have to tell me twice. I'm starving."

Everyone laughed.

As Gayla dug in, she said, "By the time he realizes he delivered them to the wrong party, the evidence will be gone."

(Laughter)

We dug into the huge appetizer platters, not knowing who ordered them, or better yet who was paying for them. I figured that cost would fall on me, but I was so busy celebrating I didn't care. No problem. After thirty minutes the huge appetizer trays still looked as though we hadn't made a dent, though we'd eaten plenty.

At one point everyone stopped eating, and I inquired, "What's wrong, why aren't you guys eating?"

Nia with a straight face, acting as though she was the spokesperson for the others said, "Oh we thought when THE QUEEN put her fork down and stopped eating that we all had to do the same, so when you put your fork down, we put ours down, too."

An absolute roar of laughter filled the room.

"Girl please, while I am a queen believe me I only put my fork down briefly and believe me I'm nowhere near finished, so you guys continue. You guys are a mess."

Nia said, "I guess when I join the royal family I'll come in throwing it down real fast, and sticking stuff in my pockets, because it's no telling when Queen Liz is gonna get full."

"Girl stop it."

Though the invitation said 6 p.m., around 7:30 just as I put a potato skin in my mouth, I felt someone tugging on my arm, when I turned around it was Shay, reeking of the same attitude she always did.

"Where am I supposed to sit?"

"What?"

"Where am I supposed to sit?"

"There are two empty seats down there Shay."

"You didn't save me a spot next to you?"

(Sigh) "No I didn't save any seats. I told people to sit wherever they wanted to."

"Who's sitting here?"

"Dy, she went to the ladies' room."

"Oh okay, I'll just move her drink and purse down there and I'll sit here."

I just about choked off of my potato skin, "Don't touch her stuff Shay, put her stuff back down. Don't you dare move her things, that's rude. She'll be right back and she's in the middle of eating her appetizers. You're an hour and a half late."

I went on to other conversations and laughing at all the pictures on the video, determined that nothing and no one would mess this evening up.

"Girl you are wrong for putting that picture of me up there. Oh my God, that's terrible. Look at my hair!"

I felt someone brush against me from behind and thought it was one of the waiters, or better yet Dy returning to her seat, but I turned and found Shay still standing there.

"Are you serious I have to sit down there?"

"Where else are you going to sit, you can't sit on someone's lap Shay? There are no seats down here."

In all honesty Shay reminded me of folks who walk in church 30-45 minutes late, waltz up to their "usual" seat in the front, and ask everyone to scoot down.

"Why can't everyone just move down one seat?"

"I'm sure they could Shay, but I'm not asking them to, so fifty people are all supposed to maneuver so you can sit down here? No, you're late. It's not happening."

I've told Shay a hundred times that she would be late to her own funeral.

Shay, huffing mad, "Are you serious?"

"I'm not asking anyone to move Shay, it started at 6 o' clock. Please don't bring that stuff in here tonight; there are two seats down there, sit there."

"I'm surprised with me being your family that you didn't save a seat for me. You knew I was coming."

"Shay!!! No I didn't know you were coming, you said you might not come, remember?"

"You should have saved me a seat just in case."

"Do you see any of my other cousins complaining?"

"I'm not worried about them; I expected a seat to be saved for me."

Shante, "Brooklyn, we can move down."

"No you can't, no one is moving anywhere."

I turned my attention back to the other conversations of reminiscing of the good ol' days, steadily stealing shots from this conversation to that conversation.

"Yeah, I couldn't believe Mr. Wood would get caught up in a situation with some young girl at the school like that."

"Well he was always flirting with us in high school, so I saw it coming."

"Well he's paying for it now."

"Whatever happened to Keith?"

"Girl, they announced at one of our last reunions that he passed away, they had his picture up on the screen and everything with others being memorialized. So, I guess he wanted to set the record straight, because he walked into our reunion last year and surprised everyone. Surprise!!!"

"Oh my goodness, you're kidding. I bet that was a surprise!"

"That's why folks shouldn't pass on every piece of information they hear. You see how folks on Facebook will post that someone passed away, yet they are alive and well. They're in such a hurry to be the first to tell it, they post stuff they haven't even verified."

"Yeah, that poor Denzel has died at least ten times."

"That's sad."

Shay finally found her way to one of the available seats, and judging from the look on her face she wasn't the least bit happy to be seated next to my ex-husband's wife.

The waiters came around and brought clean appetizer plates, "Everything okay?"

"Yes, everything is fine, thank you for taking such good care of us."

"My pleasure, we will be back for your dinner orders. I'll leave the appetizers out since I see more guests have arrived. Are you ladies enjoying yourselves?"

"Yes!!!"

The Whispers were playing in the background and I heard someone say, "Man they don't make music like that anymore."

"You got that right!"

The atmosphere and comradery made my heart melt. We really needed this.

The waiters came to take our dinners orders, and though we were well on our way to being stuffed after the appetizers, we still ordered.

"Oh don't worry about it, anything you can't eat we'll wrap up for you."

Connie, "Brook, I just want to say thanks for being the glue in bringing us all together. I know it's already been said, but I just had to say it from my mouth to your ears girl. I don't know if this would have *ever* happened if you didn't take the time to do this. Thank you so much. I'm not kidding you, it's done my heart good."

The waiter asked, "Did anyone order a diet coke?"

Evette, "Wrong table Sir, no need in ordering a diet coke with all this food, that's like folks who go to Fat Burger and get a double, double whatever with extra everything on it, and a large fry and a diet coke, why bother?"

"Girl stop. You're still a mess."

"No, she's a hot mess!"

As the salads were delivered Dawn asked everyone to bow their heads as she blessed the food, ending the prayer with, "And thank you Lord for the food we've already eaten. In Jesus' name, Amen." We all snickered because surely we'd already eaten plenty before giving thanks.

I heard some of the rude answers Shay gave from time to time to anyone who asked anything about her; very simple questions that really didn't warrant an attitude were met with rude abrupt answers. Ladies asking her what she'd been up to, or if she still worked at the bank, or if she was married were all met with much attitude. Any questions asked about Shay's kids were ignored or rudely answered as well. I didn't know what the big deal was but somewhere along the way she'd become that person who could be all up in someone else's business, but never wanting to talk about her own. But like me, they ignored her as well, not allowing anything or anyone to change the atmosphere of the evening.

Evette being one to never ever bite her tongue, but also often has a calming effect on situations, said, "Let's keep the same loving flow going, we don't have any room for negativity. It is not welcomed in here."

Shay rolled her eyes, knowing the comment was meant for her.

Having arrived earlier in the day to set up the room and tell the staff what I wanted, they quietly informed me that after they bagged up everyone's food, and replenished a few drinks they would handle the rest. They took off the video and allowed a cd of oldies and jazz to play.

Shay walked over and asked, "Are you going to play that type of music all night?"

"Yes, I plan to."

"You don't have any rap?"

"I don't listen to rap Shay, and this is my party."

"This music is boring me to death," as she headed back to her seat.

While Shay didn't like any of my birthday plans, she surely didn't like the fact that I had balloons.

"You know balloons are for kids."

"Okay, then I'll be a kid."

I didn't want to make my party all about me, as there were at least four other birthdays of other ladies within the same month as mine. I was also privy to some information regarding the sex of Kris' grandchild, so I decorated accordingly. I also had Winnie put a few graduation balloons up, as Leesa and Paula recently graduated with their degrees. As usual Winnie did an excellently job with the balloons and other decorations.

Handing the last of the to-go bags to the ladies, and tidying up the tables a bit, the waiters pushed a button which slid back and extended the room.

"Wow, that is beautiful! What's she up to now?"

"Ladies, I am so glad that you all took the time to come and share this evening with me, as I made my invite list I kept saying to myself this night wouldn't be the same without her, and I'm grateful that though months and even years have passed, and some in my Girls in My Circle group have passed on, that you took the time out of your busy schedules to make time to celebrate with me. But, it's not all about me. Anyone who knows me knows I never make it all about me. I'm sure seeing all the different colors, decorations and balloons you see it's way more than being about my birthday. We've got several things to celebrate, starting with our friendship of course."

Some of the ladies look perplexed.

"These graduation balloons and this cake are in honor of Leesa and Paula, ladies please stand. I wanted to take a second to congratulate both of you on obtaining your Master's degrees, I know it wasn't easy finishing with all the other things you're doing, but nothing worthwhile is ever easy, right? You allowed nothing to stop you from pressing forward towards your goal, no matter how long it took, no matter how many obstacles along the way. You did it! You kept plugging along while working, while raising kids, while even raising other people's kids. Yes, you did it!!! Congratulations!"

Other ladies clapped. Shay looked as if it was all no big deal.

"Jazzy, Roxie, DeeDee, Q, and Michela had birthdays last week, I'm sure you thought I forgot, this cake is in celebration of your birthdays. Happy Birthday ladies."

"Sister Lalah, please stand."

"Why's she asking me to stand up, I didn't graduate and it's not my birthday either?"

"This cake here represents you and Carl. You may think I forgot, but I know it's your anniversary tomorrow. Wow. 35 years. I salute you."

"Thank you, it hasn't been easy."

"I'm sure it hasn't been, but you stood through all of the for better and for worse, and I'm happy for you."

"By the way, Carl sent these flowers to the restaurant for you."

"Oh they're beautiful!!"

"The next cake is pink."

Evette, "Oh Lord don't tell me someone in here is pregnant."

"I hope not."

Laughter filled the room

"Toi, please stand."

"Me?"

"Yeah, you. With all the stuff already going on in your life you chose not to allow your sister's daughters to go back into the system, and recently adopted them. I honor you today in making such a choice. You were so excited when your own kids left the nest, but now you've put your own life on hold to raise someone else's. Congratulations on your new daughters. You'll surely be blessed for it all."

She teared up, "I already have been blessed. Thank you."

"The other pink cake is for you Eden, please stand. You fought breast cancer with such dignity. You never complained. You never gave up. When your hair came out all you said was, "It's just hair, it will grow back." You've been an example of strength. You've been an example of faith. I salute you!"

I watched as ladies reached for their napkins again, dabbing their eyes. I reached for one, too.

The last cake is blue...matching the balloons above it. "Ms. V. stand up?"

"Now you guys know I'm not having a baby."

"I know something you don't know, and that is that your grandchild that is still in the oven is a boy."

We watched as that girl did a dance around the room like no other dance I'd ever seen. She hollered, "Oh my God, finally a boy, after all those girls, finally a boy!!!"

I nodded to the waiters that I was finished. The candles were then put on the birthday cakes and the room belted out Stevie Wonder's version of Happy Birthday. I made a wish, blew out the candles, as did the other birthday girls.

Winnie had placed cards next to my birthday cake with a note, *Share one of your favorite quotes about friendship and place it in the box before you leave tonight.* So while the ladies were partaking in the different choices of cakes, they also jotted a little something down on the cards.

We ate cake, mingled, and before long we found ourselves in an area of the large room dancing. Gerald Albright's, "Walker's Theme" came on, and there we were in the middle of the floor doing the Gumbeaux.

Shay looked on as though we were all acting silly; as though we were old hens not acting our age, but no one seemed to care, we were having the time of our lives.

Mr. Sexy man came on and we continued on the floor, no doubt singing loud enough for other lingering patrons to hear. When the song got to the chorus we kept our steps, never missing a beat, as we laughed and sang the chorus. *Heeeeey Mr. Sexy Man, what yo name is?"*

"Girl I forgot these feet could move like this? I bet I'll feel it in the morning."

"In the morning? Girl, I feel it now!"

"I might not be able to get out of bed tomorrow."

"I'm not getting out of the bed in the morning!"

I begged, "Come on, let's do one more, one more, come on!"

"Girl you're trying to kill us tonight. This girl has taken a few line dance classes and now we can't keep her off the floor."

Biker's Shuffle came on, and I heard Bree say, "I'm gonna need some Bengay in the morning."

"Yeah, me too."

We checked the time and figured time was far spent, and we'd probably worn out our welcome.

"We'll take the check now."

"Okay, let me go get it."

The head waiter returned, again I asked, "Can we get the check? I guess we better prepare to leave before you guys throw us out of here."

"No ma'am, we don't close for another hour, you're fine. We can cut more cake, anyone want ice cream with their cake, some coffee, whatever you want?"

He took a couple of ice cream and coffee orders, and I again asked "Can you please bring the check?"

This was the time of the evening I often dreaded, but fortunately this time I was prepared to make up any difference if things with the check didn't work out, I'd even cover the cost of the appetizer trays. I hated going out on large parties and having to divvy up the bill, where inevitably someone always forgot they had a meal, three drinks, and extra this and that, and had the nerves to send down $20. It's the very reason I steered clear of large parties. How in the world someone sends down $20 when they know their meal was $19.95, and they ordered four things beyond that, I'll never understand, but, it happens all the time.

The waiter returned yet again with more cake plates, this time followed by the manager.

"Ms. Brooklyn, we would like to thank you for dining with us tonight, I hope the service was above what you expected, and that you'll consider dining with us again in the future. Thank you. Please come again ladies. It was our pleasure serving you."

Dumbfounded, I said, "Sir, but we haven't paid yet."

"I've been told to give you this and wish you a very happy birthday."

He handed me a bouquet of multi-colored roses and a card attached. I opened the card and it was from my boss.

"Wow."

"What's wrong Brook?"

"Nothing's wrong, the waiter just handed me a receipt showing our bill was paid in full."

"Are you kidding me?"

"Who would do that?"

"My boss, Mr. Latham."

"Wow that's very nice."

"Well now we know where all those appetizers came from."

I dabbed my eyes a few times, always quick to bawl at the kindness of others.

People at the other end of the table couldn't quite hear what had just transpired so Janae told them, "The waiter just told her that Brooklyn's boss paid for everything."

"Wow. My boss wouldn't bring in a box of donuts, and yours did all this. That's awesome."

Tesa smiled and said, "I don't know why she's so surprised someone did something nice for her, she's always doing so much for other people, hey, what goes around really does come around."

"Right."

I heard the soft conversations of others still commenting on how nice Mr. Latham's gesture was.

I heard Bree suggest, "Why don't we send our money down anyway, and that will be for Brooklyn's birthday."

"That's a great idea."

"Ladies please don't do that, let this be a blessing for all of us."

Shay couldn't contain herself, she must've been bursting at the seams, "I don't see why everyone is so overwhelmed about him paying the bill. He should pay it, he's rich, and he won't even miss the money, this is like a drop in a bucket for him. Plus, he's just going to write it off on his taxes, anyway."

Most of the ladies seemed stunned into silence from Shay's rude comment, and before I could respond Evette said, "That's not even the point Shay, whether he has money or not he didn't have to do it."

Toiya cut the conversation short, "Let's just leave it alone, learn to pick your battles, and this one isn't worth talking about. Let's receive it as a blessing and keep it pushing."

I felt that everyone had grown throughout the years, but Shay.

I turned to the waiters and thanked them, "We left you all some cake, thanks for everything." They embraced me as though we were long time buddies.

Before leaving I asked Ms. Gouche' to sing a song. I'd heard her sing many times before when we were younger. It seemed so appropriate having grown up with her and being one of the girls in my circle that she sing a little somethin' somethin'. She closed us out with "Thank You," by Walter Hawkins. The room was loud and full of praise. *It could have been me outdoors, with no food, no clothes, no friend…or just another number, with a tragic end.* Ladies were all into it, swaying, dancing, waving their arms, and hitting their chest, as if personalizing the song to their own lives. Jackie sang the chorus again, *It could've been me outdoors…* We all sang along, at times the actual soloist was totally drowned out. Jackie balled her fist as a choir director would do to show the song was ending and closed us out with our finally line, *Thank you Lord for all you've done for me.*

We clapped, hugged, laughed, dabbed our eyes as we left the room. Most of us still humming and singing the song as we made our way through the restaurant...*but you didn't see fit to let any of these things be. Thank you Lord.*

Don't judge a man til' you've walked a mile in his shoes, after that who cares, you're a mile away and you have his shoes.

People who judge others speak volumes about how they feel about themselves.

Enjoy life by limiting your emotional baggage to a tiny carry-on.

It's the friends we meet along the way who help us appreciate the journey.

Things are never quite as scary when you've got a best friend.

Good friends care for each other; close friends understand each other. But true friends are there beyond words, distance or time for each other.

CHAPTER

Five

We made our way out to the valet parking booth, "Good evening ladies, I hope you had a good time."

"Yes Sir, we had a great time, thanks."

"I'll take your tickets. This is a large crowd, please be patient with us as we get your cars, and those of other patrons before you."

I responded, "No problem, it gives us more time to catch up and laugh some more, and of course take more pictures."

I watched as Donna continuously snapped pictures on her camera. She'd been that way since school, the one always capturing the moments, even at times when we didn't want the moments captured.

I looked down at all the gifts I received, and said, "So much for your presence is gift enough."

Evette responded, "Girl please, have we ever listened to you?"

Shay stepped away from the group and was talking on her cell phone, I got her attention. "He's taking all of our parking tickets, give him your ticket."

"I didn't valet park."

"No? So where'd you park?"

"I took Uber here; I'm riding home with you."

"So, it never crossed your mind to check with me regarding my plans, and if I had room for someone to ride with me?"

"Nope."

I sighed. "Common courtesy would have been to tell me of your arrangements Shay, you hadn't a clue if I rode with someone else tonight, after all it is my birthday celebration, and others did offer to pick me up."

"Well, it's not like it's that far out of the way for you. You can jump back on the freeway after you drop me off."

"It is out of the way, and it's always about you Shay, isn't it?"

She giggled a bit, and said, "Haven't you figured that out yet? Yes, it's always about me?"

Evette gently touched my shoulder and whispered, "Brooklyn don't let this ruin your night, it's been such a lovely evening. I can't wait til' we get together again."

I turned to Shay, "I'm not in my SUV Shay, I don't know how this is going to work, you're going to have to hold some of this stuff."

"Or, I can drive and you can hold it."

"That's not happening."

If I didn't watch so much of the Discovery ID channel I would have let her find whatever way home she could, but I didn't want anything to happen to her. I couldn't live with that. She may not care about others, but I do care about her.

The valet brought the car up, and commenced to putting all of the gifts into the trunk of my little two-seater. This wasn't an easy fete considering the things already in the trunk. There were so many gifts I, along with a few other ladies, decided to hand boxes and bags to the valet to alleviate him from having to walk back and forth, all while Shay sat in the passenger seat offering no assistance.

The valet asked, "Ma'am, where would you like us to put this cake box and these other gifts, nothing else will fit in the trunk?"

I walked up to the passenger side of the car and asked Shay if she could hold the cake and some gifts. She reacted as though I asked her to do far more than hold a few gifts and a cake box, but finally answered me in a tone that made me feel as though I was inconveniencing her, when in fact I was the one inconvenienced by her.

Shay grunted, "I guess so, if I have to."

The valet closed Shay's door, and walked me around to the driver's side where he closed my door as well. I strapped myself in and was about to pull off, when I realized I hadn't tipped the valet.

"Oh, wait a minute sir, I'm sorry. I want to give you something."

Shay being Shay just had to say something, "I don't know why you're tipping him; he's only doing his job. Who else do they expect to go get the car for you?"

The valet totally ignored Shay's comment, just as I had, and simply said, "Thank you very much, drive safely, and Happy Birthday!"

"Wow that was fun, I haven't had that much fun in a long time, and it was so good to see everyone. I'm getting to believe that *black don't crack stuff*, the ladies looked awesome."

Shay just about bit my head off, "Everyone looked awesome, really? Are you serious? I thought a few of them looked a hot mess."

I didn't want to hear any of Shay's negativity so I continued driving in silence. But, the silence proved to be too much for Shay to handle because after about five minutes she talked non-stop.

"You enjoyed that?"

"Yes, I sure did."

"That was pretty uneventful for a 50th birthday to me. And, I don't see why you thought it was such a big deal that Mr. Latham paid for everything; that's the least he can do, he's oozing of money. You practically run the company anyway. He won't even miss that little change. I just don't see what the big deal was about him paying."

Shaking my head, I responded, "I can't believe you said that. Who can't see how nice of a gesture that was? You know, people don't have to do things for you. And, by the way, it doesn't matter how much money he has, the fact is, he didn't have to do it. He didn't have to feed me and surely didn't have to feed nearly fifty of my friends and family."

"I didn't need him to feed me, but it's called a "write-off" Brooklyn."

"Whatever it's called, he didn't have to do it. I didn't need him to feed me either, I have money too, but that's not the point. None of us needed him to feed us, we all came prepared to pay, but it's nice that he thought to do such a nice thing."

"Yeah I'm sure some of those broke heifers were glad they didn't have to pay, they were probably spending their lunch money for next week."

This would be the beginning of a very long eight mile ride home with Shay. I found myself sighing and praying with every push of the pedal.

"You know it ticked me off that you didn't save a seat for me. I know you all do all that "sister" stuff, but I'm blood."

"Shay, you were late. If you didn't notice you were an hour and a half late."

"And? You still should have saved my seat."

"You always try to complicate things all the time, and you're always late."

"I'm always late, if you haven't figured it out yet I operate on my time, and no one else's. Plus, quite honestly the party doesn't usually start til' I get there."

"Yeah okay, sorry to burst your bubble, but the party started way before then."

I took a glance over at Shay in disbelief that someone's mouth could really move so much. The girl was hardly taking breaths in between all the insults of others. She seemed oblivious to my annoyance, but then again she probably didn't care.

In normal Shay form she commenced to pick apart everyone who was at the party.

"What was that Camille had on? I don't think people realize how ridiculous they look with those fake eye lashes on, at least try to make them look natural. Dang, those girls went to college for over twenty years, how long does it take to finish college? You can't tell me Donna's husband isn't cheating on her; she sure doesn't fix herself up at all. I can't believe Sharice has yet another husband, that's the craziest thing in the world, folks who look like something like me can't find a good man and look at her, she's already remarried. She looks a mess. I remember how her feet were always ashy, looked like sand paper. Why does Jeanie walk like that? Tiffany can't be clean with those long nails, man that's nasty. I wonder how she wipes herself, or cleans her house. What's wrong with Gayle's eye? Did Lina have a weight loss surgery, she looks sick? I thought you said Yolanda lost weight, she must've found it again. You know when people get a certain age they should lessen the amount of make-up they wear, Teresa looked like a clown, I think they call that "casket ready.""

I sighed.

She continued, "I think Tisha broke a few hair rules, I'm sure you're not supposed to put a curly hair piece on nappy hair. What was up with Shanna's hair, so she shaved off her hair then glues a fake piece up there, that's not cute. No, that's not cute at all."

She busted up laughing at her own self. She continued.

"They sure did a lot of talking about their degrees, who gives a rat's butt about their degrees. It hasn't gotten them anywhere. Sheree is still at the bank, in the same position she was in twenty years ago, every time I see her she's waiting on a position to come available, so what has a degree done for her? Looks like Mika had some sort of plastic surgery."

I continued to drive stone faced, no expression, no laughter, no comment, while Shay thought things she said were totally hilarious.

"And Deborah cracks me up with all that don't call me DEBRA stuff, my name is DE-BO-RAH. Whatever. Girl you're from the hood, it's DEBRA."

I finally spoke, "Did you forget you changed your name, too?"

"Oh you finally said something, you've been so quiet."

"Yes, you've been talking so much how could I say anything?"

"Well I was just making conversation because you weren't talking."

"Did you notice that Louis Vuitton purse Marva was carrying; now you know that's probably a knock off? I was pretty surprised to hear that Tonya was a prisoner. What did she do? Ain't no tellin'."

"Who said she was a prisoner Shay?"

"I don't recall who said it, but someone was asking why she didn't come tonight, and someone said she was a prisoner."

"She's not in prison Shay. She's not a prisoner; she works in a prison as a prison nurse. You will always flip something to the negative won't you? You'll always hear what you want to hear. You've gone on non-stop criticizing every single lady there tonight. Does it make you feel better to tear people down Shay to make yourself feel better? Does it help build you up? You couldn't find one good thing about anyone there tonight. But guess what, you can't put makeup on the inside and cover it up like you do the outside. You can get all the Mac and Lancome in the world and it won't work on the inside Shay. Do you remember what Uncle James used to say?"

"What?"

"You can make ugly look better with some makeup, but it can't mask a bad attitude."

She rolled her eyes, but of course I continued.

"You spent most of this ride home talking about the other ladies. They looked beautiful. That's the good part about it all, we can be different colors and shades, sizes, have different views and we're still beautiful. I love those ladies; it's a lot of stories to tell between all of us. If we were all the same it would be one boring night wouldn't it?"

"It was boring to me anyway."

"Well you could have left at any time."

She blurted out, "Girl, please tell me why Connie would put on that onesie. I swear I didn't know they made onesies that big."

"I thought she looked beautiful. She accessorized it beautifully, and the cover-up piece she had on with it was amazing, the colors were so bright and pretty."

"Girl please."

"You know people don't have to look like you to be beautiful Shay."

"Well they sure don't look like me, that's for sure."

As we pulled up to Shay's house I continued talking, I felt it was my turn now, "Oh and by the way, if you want some of the answers to all those questions you spewed out let me answer them for you."

I didn't take the time to call out everyone's name; I just spewed out answers to all the questions I could remember.

"She walks like that because she had a stroke. Oh and she walks like that because she walks on a prosthesis. She lost part of her leg in an accident, but guess who had the loudest laugh in the room tonight? She did, because she's been through a horrible situation, and is grateful to be alive. Oh, let me move on to all of your other questions. Oh, her hair is cut like that because that's how she likes to wear it. And, her husband must like it; he's still with her 30 years later. Let me see who else you asked about, oh, yeah, she does look sick, but guess what? She just finished chemo and cared enough about all of us to come out tonight to spend the evening with us for my birthday. And by the way, this was a celebration for her to just be able to get out again. As for the degrees, they didn't give up Shay, no matter how long it took them they didn't give up. Hey, it's better to have a degree and not need it than to need it and not have it. Right?"

"Whatever."

"And, by the way, her eyes are like that because she has a thyroid problem. Anything else you want to know Sheila?"

"Don't call me that."

Somehow I always reverted back to her given name when I got fed up with her.

"Oh, and so what if someone's purse is a knock off if that's what she wants to carry. Look at all the folks who pay $3,000 for one of those purses and only have five dollars in it."

"Well I hope you're not talking about me with that comment, I have money in mine."

"You know what Shay you've become more and more difficult to be around. If you're not complaining you're talking about someone, and it has worn me and everyone else out. People don't like being around you."

"Well they don't have to be, I don't need anyone. I told you I don't do women anyway."

"We all need someone Shay."

"You might, but I sure as hell don't. Speak for yourself."

"You remember how Barb didn't like her son in law for years. She could not stand that man; just the sight of him irritated her. But, guess who was there for her before she passed? It wasn't her son, nor her daughter, it was the son in law she disliked so much. There he was taking her to appointments, feeding her, bathing her, sitting there all day every day with the hospice nurses. He even kept a log of when he'd given her medicine and when the next round was due."

"And I care about this why?"

"I'm trying to say you need to stop saying you don't need anyone, because let me tell you, you never know what life has in store...none of us know that. The very person you don't like and think you never needed, might be the one you need."

"Girl please."

I asked, "So you're telling me a room with nearly 50 women you couldn't find one good thing to say about any of them?"

"Not one."

"So have you ever heard if you have nothing good to say don't say anything at all?"

She rolled her eyes.

"You talk about Deborah's appearance all the time. She hasn't changed, she's dressed and looked like that for years, and as over the top as it may be to others, guess who was the first one there for you when your father passed? Guess who will give you the shirt off her back in a heartbeat?"

"I don't know, but I'm sure you're going to tell me."

"Yep. Deborah. She was the one cooking, cleaning, serving folks, but none of your other "friends" lifted a finger. All I'm trying to tell you is that you need to start seeing the inner beauty of people, instead of always critiquing the outside. You can't always judge a book by its cover; and while you're at it work on yourself."

"Oh, I'm sorry I'm not as perfect as you and your little girls in your circle group."

"Girl please, there's nothing perfect about any of us, and we'll all be the first to tell you that, don't ever get that twisted. Well let me speak for myself, I'm not perfect, and if the girls in my circle group consisted of only perfect folks then I surely would have to end my membership."

"You act like all those females care about you, and they're just a bunch of phony heifers."

"What's phony about them Shay?"

"They just are."

"Yeah, that's what you say when you have nothing else to say. You're just jealous, and have never learned to share me with others. You can't stand that I'm close to other females. The only reason you don't like those women is because you don't want to like them. They've done nothing to you. Have you ever thought about the fact that each one of those ladies bring something different to the table?"

"Oh here you go."

"Here I go what Shay?"

"About to preach."

"No, actually I'm just letting you know that you can have more than one good friend because they all bring something different. What one of them will do with me, another won't. For instance, I'll never get Nessa to go on a marathon walk with me, but she'll go to the spa; yet Ronna won't go to the spa, she'll go to the jazz concerts. Marvelyn won't go to the jazz concert, so she's the one I'll see Frankie Beverly with. And, Treena's crazy butt has been trying to get me to go backpack hiking, and that's not happening so she'll have to grab someone else for that. Also, you can talk to different friends about different things, so it's pretty nice, just because you're doing something with one more often than the other doesn't diminish the love you have for anyone else."

"Whatever. I don't trust any of them."

"Let me ask you this Shay, since you've taken the time to pick every single person apart tonight, I'm just curious if you want to know any good things about them? Do you want to know about any of the organizations these ladies volunteer their time to, or better yet, the organizations they started? Do you want to know about their service to others? Do you want to know about the ones who are raising family members who aren't their own kids? Did you want to hear about the ones who hit rock bottom, but came back on top? Did you want to hear about the ones who've had medical issues throughout the years, but kept plugging along?"

"No, not really. Are you done?"

"No I'm not done Shay. It kills you when you're not the one talking and you don't have the stage, but no I'm not finished."

"I am."

"I'm not. You know what Shay, the only one there tonight who hasn't grown is you. You've been through some things and you decided to park right there in your piss off. It's like you're walking around with all this baggage that you won't put down. You choose to stay bitter. You choose to stay mad at whoever hurt you, and take it out on everyone else that crosses your path. How is that right?"

"It just is."

"It's not Shay. You need to stop. You've been walking around for years mad. You're mad in the morning, you're mad in the afternoon, you're mad at night, you're mad every day, you're mad when you wake up, you're mad when you go to bed, you're just mad. You were mad when you were married, you're mad when you're single. What is it Shay? You're bitter over everything, as though you're the only one to have been hurt. Well guess what, you'll have to get in line and take a number with that one."

"What?"

"I said you need to get in line and take a number if you want to tell your story of being hurt by your relationships. We all have a story Shay. We can all line up and tell a story, but you want to act like you're the lone ranger. We've all been hurt. We've all had challenges, but how long do you stay down? How long do you stay mad? All you're doing is letting someone else win when they get you so mad it takes you out of your character the way it has. This is not the favorite cousin I knew. You've changed so much. Do you remember what Gramby used to say Shay?"

"What now Brook, what did Gramby say now?"

"You've got two choices, getting up or giving up…and giving up wasn't an option so you really only have one choice."

"Where's your comeback Shay?"

"My what?"

"You know what Gramby used to say, you have to have some *comeback*. It's when you get up and dust your butt off and get back in the game. Like when fighters fight, they go into their corners, re-group and get back in the ring. You never re-grouped, you stayed in the corner. You need to get back in the game. It's always going to be things in life that blindside you, you're not the lone ranger with breakups Shay, we've all been hurt, and probably hurt folks ourselves, and while you may not like how things ended, it is what it is. Have you ever heard that when things don't work out it's because there's someone or something better for you? Well how about look forward to that? You want to talk about how that ex-boyfriend of yours texted you to break up with you, and as cowardly as that may be, at least you got that. My ex stopped accepting calls and texts, played a Casper and straight disappeared, but we can't park there. Let them go! Let it go! Hey, sometimes you can even thank them for doing you a favor. Regardless, we've got to keep moving. But again Shay, we all have a story. If everyone told their story tonight we'd still be at the restaurant. We all have a story! You're not the first one divorced twice, you're not the first one who wanted something different in a relationship, you're not the only one who has been blindsided, and you're not the only one who tried to see something in someone that wasn't there. You're mad at this relationship, you're mad at this promotion, but you never ever look at the fact that each job you wanted and tested for was eventually cut in the budget, so why not see the blessing in that instead of being mad?"

"You know Brooklyn, I really don't care."

"I'm not saying what someone did to you was right, I'm just saying you should reach that point where you're not going to let it bother you anymore, honestly that's the blessing in it, *that it doesn't bother you anymore.*

"Are you finished preaching your sermon? Good ol' church girl always has a sermon."

"No one is preaching a sermon Shay. I'm just talking to my cousin."

"Yes you are, and you're judging me, I thought the good ol' church folks weren't supposed to judge others."

"No I'm not judging you at all. I'm just saying that in life we have choices, and if you choose to continue with all your antics and attitude, I can choose not to be around it, but I really do love you."

"Suit yourself."

Shay grabbed her purse and opened the car door, "Are you done?"

Before I knew it she had slammed my door and headed to her front door.

Never judge people on the opinions of others.

Counting other people's sins does not make you a saint.

True friends are never apart, maybe in distance, but never in heart.

If you want to find out who is a true friend, screw up or go through a challenging time, and then see who sticks around.

Good friends are like stars, you don't always see them, but you know they're always there.

CHAPTER

Six

I noticed the seats roped off when I entered the church, but didn't think much of it. I figured someone was having a family reunion where many of their family members wanted to worship together before heading back to their respective hometowns. No doubt they'll probably come in dressed alike in family reunion t-shirts, but just maybe they'd come in suited and booted, sharp as a tack. Regardless, I needed to find another seat because my usual seat was roped off.

An usher approached me, "I saw all the pictures and videos on Facebook of your birthday dinner last night, looks like you all had a ball."

"Yes ma'am, we had a great time, but I'm going to need some toothpicks to keep my eyes opened this morning. We even tried to get up and do a little dancing, but I'm paying for it right now. I've got stuff hurting on me I didn't know I had."

We laughed.

The usher beckoned me to come forward, "Come on up here to your regular seat, you don't look right sitting back there."

"No it's roped off. I'm good."

"You can sit here."

"No it's obviously being reserved for someone. I'm good."

"Girl get up here. I'm taking down the rope for this row now."

I moved up to the third row, and started digging in my purse for my phone to pay my tithes online, gone are the days of writing checks, at least for me. But, I must admit it does feel a bit funny walking by the offering table and putting nothing in it.

Pastor Clark walked to the podium at exactly 9 o'clock, "I'm going to wait a few minutes and allow people to take their seats; it's a lot of movement still going on, lots of folks still coming in. Praise God. Let's prepare for worship."

He held onto both sides of the podium, and softly sang along as the musicians played, *Mighty are the works of your hands.*

I began singing to the music. *Your name is above all names.*

I lifted my hands in praise; tears formed in my eyes remembering the last time I heard that song my hands were lifted signifying HELP, now PRAISE! I opened my eyes to find an usher standing by me, "I didn't want to interrupt you, but I wanted to hand you this, Happy Birthday."

She gave me a gentle hug as she continued to her post. I totally appreciated how she waited until I opened my eyes, and didn't interrupt my worship. I've never understood how people, especially those who are late, disrupt someone's worship instead of waiting to be seated.

I sat the bag down next to me, but then the usher returned and said, "You can open it now."

After pulling out the lavender tissue paper I found a journal. I looked up at the usher and thanked her, and told her it was a perfect gift because I love to write. She told me to reach inside the bag some more where I found a few chocolate goodies, and a t-shirt with the words GIRLS IN MY CIRCLE written in silver on the front.

Glitter had never really been my thing, often people put so much glitter on stuff til' it looks ghetto fabulous to me, but this was definitely a high quality shirt with elegance.

I smiled. "Thank you, you didn't have to do this."

"Yes, I did. Happy Birthday. Enjoy the service!"

I figured because she made t-shirts for many church events that she saw my birthday pictures on Facebook and decided to make me one. How nice.

I jumped when someone got close to my ear and sang, *Thank you for being a friend,* the same song from the birthday party. I looked up and it was Evette with her crazy self.

"What are you doing here?"

Before she could answer I heard all this movement behind me, and turned to see a sea of ladies in lavender shirts, like mine.

I covered my mouth in shock, "You've got to be kidding me!!!"

I was so surprised tears filled my eyes.

"Go head and cry, crybaby."

I laughed through the tears that were trying not to fall.

"You guys got me good. You're going to make me mess up my makeup."

A few others who couldn't make the dinner the previous night were in tow and tears flowed at the sight of them.

Some hugged me as they hurried to their seats.

"Are you kidding me? Oh my goodness, tell me that's not Janine from elementary school."

She hugged me very quickly and kept moving to her seat, "Yes, it sure is. Gotcha!!"

"I want to put my t-shirt on too."

Tara said, "Hurry, just slide it over your head."

Service started and truly I was overwhelmed. Those I didn't have time to speak to got my attention and waved. I turned and saw some of the ladies from my high school journalism class. I mouthed, "Noooo way."

Some brought their husbands and children, and I turned to Evette and said, "Who did you threaten to get all these folks here this morning?"

She laughed.

Takim took the mic, and started singing one of my favorite songs. I closed my eyes and sang along, *I really love the Lord, you don't know what He's done for me, gave me the victory.*

I heard Mother Drew shout from behind, "I know fo' myself what the Lord will do, I know fo' myself!!!"

With my hands lifted in praise, I felt someone hit me rather hard on my shoulder. I opened my eyes, and had to bend down to see who it was under this very huge hat. It was Shay.

"Scoot over; I want to sit on the end."

I moved out of my row into the aisle to let Shay in, as she continued to protest that she wanted to sit on the end.

"What's that on your head?"

"A hat."

"When did you start wearing hats?"

"The preacher likes hats doesn't he?"

"Don't start Shay. Don't bring your nonsense in here."

"I bet you didn't expect to see me did you?"

"No I didn't, actually I'm totally surprised; I didn't expect to see any of you guys. I can't believe no one let this secret slip. But you're right, I didn't expect to see you."

I really didn't expect to see quite a few of the ladies that came, as Gramby used to call them CME members, the ones who only come on Christmas, Mother's Day and Easter, and of course this wasn't either of those days.

"Well any excuse to come here, I'm still trying to get the good Reverend's attention."

"Shay don't start."

"I told you he's married."

Thinking she was being humorous, and not caring if he was married or not, she replied, "Amen."

I sighed and got back into the service.

Before long I looked up and Shay was standing up, waving her arms and clapping her hands, reminded me of those people who fall asleep through the entire sermon and when the Pastor gets to whoopin' they're the first ones standing and waving their hands. Sorry but that just cracks me up, you were sleep! You didn't even hear the sermon.

Shay's attention was drawn to a lady who started shouting, she tapped me on the shoulder and leaned over and asked, "Does it really take all of that?"

I looked at her and said, "Obviously it does for her Shay, you don't know what her praise is about."

Looking at yet another lady Shay leaned over, "I can't believe she wore that to church, even I know better than that."

Oh here she goes about to rip everyone apart in the church as she did with all the ladies at my birthday dinner.

"She's fine Shay, that's how we dress here, if you look around you're the only one with a lampshade on your head."

She rolled her eyes.

Pastor Clark followed the scripture with a prayer, Shay talked during the beginning of the prayer until I finally told her to be quiet, but I did catch the end, "Lord, I thank you that the four walls of my bedroom last night were not the four walls of a hospital room, or the four walls of a casket. It tells me you have more work for me to do. I thank you Lord that things are as well as they are. In Jesus' name, Amen."

I couldn't believe it, but somehow Shay managed to be quiet during the sermon. At some points it appeared the Pastor had even struck a nerve with her. As Pastor Clark made it towards the end of his sermon entitled "Baggage," saying some of the things I'd already told Shay, she shuffled in her seat a bit, she seemed a bit uncomfortable.

"If I can get a few Amens up in here I might go ahead and wrap this up, you know when you're quiet I preach longer."

The congregation laughed, and many said "AMEN" very loud.

Laughing, Pastor Clark continued, "You guys aren't right. But, getting back to my sermon, some of us are walking around with so much baggage it's worse than that hoarding show. I was watching last week's show and a lady couldn't throw away a shoe box full of old lottery tickets. Now, mind you, they were losing tickets, but she couldn't throw them away. What are you holding onto in your life that needs to be thrown out?"

He paused and walked across the pulpit.

"Again I ask, what are you holding onto that needs to be tossed from your life? What baggage are you lugging around with you? Aren't you tired of carrying all that? What's weighing you down? Mental? Physical? Financial? What is it that you lug around with you every single day? Wouldn't things be lighter for you if you unpacked all that stuff? Oh I know on the show they have anxiety about getting rid of things like furniture, trinkets, clothing, and for sure that's baggage. And, if you've ever watched the show you can see where much in their living situation stinks due to their hoarding. But, we too have some things that stink and we need to rid ourselves of it. How about that bad attitude? It stinks. How about that bitterness? It stinks. How about that racism? Man, does that stink. Oh let's not forget jealousy, yeah, that stinks too. Oh it may not be that you've bought too much of something at the store, and that your house and garage and cars are overflowing with clutter, but let me ask you this, is your mind cluttered? Is your life cluttered? I'd say that's baggage. Is it past hurts? Trust issues? Is it the unforgiving spirit you have? Are you determined to hold that grudge til' you die? Is it your judgmental attitude towards others? Had some losses you couldn't overcome? Still carrying some rejection around with you? Have you made some errors in judgment? It's all baggage. Oh my goodness, let me raise my own hand on that one, I've had some lapses in judgment myself, whew, and you guys probably thought I was up here just preaching to you, no, preaching to myself too."

"Amen."

"Tell me, is it that unloving spirit you carry around with you? Just like all the stuff they show in the houses of hoarders on this show isn't pretty, our stuff is not pretty either. It's all baggage. Your suitcase is overflowing with junk; weighing you down, and you've lugged it around so long you don't know how to let it go. Let it go!!! Grab on to things that are worth holding onto, and let the rest go! Shoot, even folks at the airport are smart enough to put stuff down when it gets too heavy, and that's what you need to do today, put it down! Can I get a few deacons to help me with this?"

When I looked up from taking my notes the minister and three deacons were trying to pull two huge suitcases to the middle of the pulpit. He pulled the zipper around to expose what was in the suitcases, and it was a bunch of cement blocks. Each block had a paper wrapped around it with a rubber band. Pastor Clark started holding up some of the blocks.

"See we carry a lot of things around with us unnecessarily. Look at this."

Each time he reached inside of the suitcase he exposed another block's message.

"Jealousy. Anger. Bitterness. Resentment. Low self-esteem. Procrastination."

Sister Bailey, "Whew, that's me Pastor. Procrastination."

"Well at least you know what it is and can work on it. God bless you Sister Bailey for being brave enough to admit it."

He continued digging the blocks out of the suitcase and calling out the label on each block. "Fear. Depression. Worry. Betrayal. Grudges. Financial burden. Relationship hurts. Divorce. Jealousy. Guilt. Stress. Insecurities. Shame. Hangups. Habits. Yeah, these bags are getting lighter already."

More congregants stood as different blocks were pulled out of the suitcases. "Now see I'm just calling out the ones I have labeled here, I bet you all have a whole bunch more you could put in this suitcase, whatever it is, unload it. Let it go!! Believe me I've got some stuff I need to unload, too. Glory to God!"

He reached down to get the last block out of the suitcase, and held it up, "UNFORGIVENESS."

Congregants grunted, as though he'd touched a nerve.

I'm just curious, "How much would the airlines charge you for your extra baggage?"

I repeated what he said, "Wow, how much would the airlines charge you for your extra baggage?"

Pastor Clark, "I'm going to go ahead and close, but I was listening to the radio the other day, and they played a beautiful song. It spoke of God giving second chances. But, if I were to be honest I'll have to admit that I used up my second chance a long time ago. But, glory to God, He's a God of more than just second chances. My word for you today is to unload the baggage, and give yourself a chance of a less burdened down life, free yourself of some things that are weighing you down. Life is short. You know what I've found? The hardest person to forgive sometimes is you."

He seemingly paused to allow his words to sink in.

"Before the benediction I'd like to say a prayer. If you have some things weighing you down come on down to the altar or stand where you are, there's no reason in us leaving with the same baggage we came with."

"Amen."

Jyon began singing, *No more shackles, no more chains, I am free, yeah*, and Pastor Clark led us in prayer.

I thought I saw a few tears forming in Shay's eyes, but when she saw me looking at her she said, "What are you looking at?"

I prayed she was touched in some way just as I was, no doubt, I too had some baggage I needed to dump.

After church I was told that some of my longtime friends wanted to take me out, I assumed those who didn't make the dinner the previous night wanted to break bread together. Truth be told all that dancing and being up late wore me out, my mind was on one thing and one thing only, going home, warming up those leftovers and falling out.

"I was going to eat my leftovers and nap all day; I'm exhausted from last night."

"Well you won't be doing that today, girl this is your birthday weekend!"

"Where are we going? I need to go home and change."

Jacque held up a pair of my jeans, "Don't worry, your mom brought me a pair of jeans to church this morning, just slip them on with your t-shirt. You know you look crazy with that t-shirt over that dress."

"Seriously, where are we going?"

"That's for us to know and you to find out."

"Yep, we're going to grab something to eat, and then make one more stop."

"One more stop where? If I'm not mistaking this is called kidnapping."

"Call it what you want sistah. Come on, hurry, the bus is pulling up, go change your clothes right quick."

"Bus?"

I turned around and saw an absolutely beautiful black charter bus, and was it clean.

"Are you serious? A bus? Ok, who's all going?"

"All of us."

"Oh my goodness, what are you guys up to?"

"Come on, hurry up girl."

I hurriedly ran to the ladies' lounge to change clothes, and said a few goodbyes to church members I passed on my way back to the bus, all while the kidnap crew kept waving and telling me to hurry up. Upon returning to the bus the driver extended his hand to help me up the steps. Winnie, asked everyone on board to join hands with someone. The bus driver stood back, but Winnie turned to him, and said, "Come on up here, we are definitely going to include you in this prayer, so you can get us to and from our destination safely."

Many of the ladies said, "Amen."

The best driver thanked everyone for the prayer and gave a few emergency instructions.

I asked the bus driver, "So, where are we going?"

He started to answer me but Evette and a few other ladies on the bus shushed him.

Evette said, "Good try Brooklyn."

Tamar said, "We'll give her the blindfolds after we leave the restaurant and get on the freeway. We better get going; they're expecting us at 2 o'clock."

Puzzled, I asked, "Blindfolds?"

Within the hour I found myself seated at a restaurant with my most favorite dish in front of me. Gumbo.

"Well girls, I don't know where we're going after this, but you're really going to have to step it up to outdo the food we just ate. I swear I can eat gumbo every single day."

"Give her the blindfolds."

Bree put the blindfolds on me, and I felt all the winding and turning of the bus, all while enjoying jazz blaring through the speakers…crystal clear I might add. The bus driver put on some oldies and we all belted out the words to the top of our lungs, "*Drifting on a memory, ain't no place I'd rather be…*"

Toya said, "Sang y'all."

It seemed with each song played, we got louder and louder.

"Girl they don't make music like that anymore. Music meant something then."

"You got that right."

I again asked, "Anyone want to tell me where we're going?"

They all continued their conversations, totally ignoring me. Quite honestly much of what I was hearing was quite similar to my birthday dinner; more laughter, more remember when stories, more questions of have you seen this person and that person from school, but mostly more clarification that we needed this time together.

Finally about thirty minutes later, the bus driver announced, "We're here."

I went to take off my blindfolds when I was told, "No not yet."

They guided me from the parking lot to the elevator to the location that held the surprise. They made sure to tell others on the elevator, "She doesn't know why she's here."

I heard a man say, "Well she'll enjoy this."

"I will, where am I?"

He ignored me too.

I listened to all the different conversations hoping I could get an inkling of what this was all about. It was totally out of my comfort zone to not know where I was going, but I went along with it. One guy obviously had an itinerary of future events for this location, but as he read it aloud to his wife he said nothing that helped me any.

"Okay, she's on this row. Scoot down Brooklyn, we got you, it's clear, just scoot down."

I scooted and scooted until someone told me to sit. I took a second to thank God for vision and not having to be escorted around like this all the time. Oh the things we take for granted.

"Can I take these things off now?"

"Yeah go ahead."

I slid the blindfolds off and could tell I was at the winery where I had seen jazz artists before.

"Oh we're here to see Boney James, huh?"

"No Brooklyn."

"Gerald Albright?"

"Girl no, you don't have to see the same two artists every time you go to a concert."

Finally the lights went out; I waited for the MC to come over the speaker and introduce the artist, instead music played without any introduction.

"Oh my God, no you guys didn't."

I got up, turned and looked one way, then the other.

"No you guys didn't, are you serious?" I kept turning around. Someone read my bucket list on Facebook, huh?"

No one answered me.

"Oh my God. Is it Frank McComb?"

"How do you know who it is, it might be musicians just playing his song?"

"No seriously is it Frank McComb?"

I looked again and saw Frank coming through the aisles of the crowd singing "Another Day." I started singing louder than him. *I must have the heart of a lion, to make it to another day.*

Frank passed right in front of me making his way to the stage, he waved in our direction and said, "Good evening Girls in My Circle."

"Oh no he didn't." I started hitting Evette on her arm like school girls did when they were excited about the Jackson 5. "Oh no he didn't say Girls in my Circle, how does he know about us?"

Frank made his way to the stage and welcomed and thanked everyone in the audience for coming out and supporting his concert. He then paused and asked all the ladies from Girls In My Circle to stand. I couldn't believe it. Everyone stood up except Shay.

I turned to her and said, "Stand up Shay, he asked us to stand."

"I don't want to stand up."

"Why didn't you wear your t-shirt?"

"I told you I don't like looking like other women, so I didn't want to wear it."

"Is it really that big of a deal Shay?"

"It is to me."

I left well enough alone, I had better things to do than to worry about Shay. Frank had been on my bucket list for a long time, and nothing was going to stop me from hearing him sing and tickle that ivory.

When I first heard of Frank McComb I loved him because the songs I heard then sounded just like Donny Hathaway, but now I loved Frank for Frank and right about now I was ecstatic to be sitting on this first row enjoying his music.

Frank looked at a few papers on his piano.

"Good evening, how's everyone doing? God bless y'all. Thanks for coming out tonight. I know in this big beautiful city there are a lot of choices you could have made tonight, but you chose to be here with me. I love coming to L.A. I see a sea of lavender shirts in the first few rows. Thank you so much Girls in My Circle for coming out tonight."

We waved, giggled and clapped, and acted like 17 year olds.

"Where's Ms. Brooklyn?" I just about peed my pants.

Evette pointed her finger and said, "She's right here."

"How about you come on up and we sing Happy Birthday to you?"

In amazement and being a little bashful, I said, "Are you serious?"

I wondered how I'd make my way on to the stage with my knees shaking the way they were, but I managed.

Frank went into a version of Happy Birthday like only he could. I thanked him and headed back to my seat.

"She's in a hurry; I was hoping you'd stay up here a little longer, sit here on the piano."

I looked at my friends in the audience while steadily giggling. Frank went into one of my favorites, "Love, Love, Love, one of Donny's oldies, but surely a goodie.

"Thank you Brooklyn, have a great birthday. Do you have any requests for us tonight?"

I had plenty of requests, but I'm sure he couldn't do them all. I found the words to speak, "How about, "Morning Glory" and "Gotta Find My Way."

"You got it!"

I made my way to my seat as the audience in this very quaint outside theatre applauded. I waved a "thank you" to everyone and sat down, as the band played "Morning Glory."

"You ladies really got me tonight. I was so tired when we left the church and ate, but I forgot all about being tired when I heard Frank McComb. You are so sneaky. I have enjoyed you all this weekend, you don't have a clue how much. I sure hope we can keep it going. I know life gets busy, but maybe we can plan something every few months or so. It doesn't have to be anyone's birthday or anything, we'll call it our "Just Because" time. I can't think of the last time I had this much fun. Thank you so much. It kind of took me back to the way we hung out after games in high school."

We wound down the hills and roads making our way back to the church. Some ladies tried to fall asleep but I was talking too much. Leisha walked through the bus allowing ladies to partake in the fruit and cheese trays that they'd stored on the bus.

"Looks like you girls thought of everything, huh?"

Leisha then doubled back and quietly asked everyone if they wanted to give towards a gratuity for the bus driver. It was agreed upon that each lady would give at least five dollars.

The ride back was a bit quieter, I think, like me, others were exhausted too. I was glad to finally see the church in view, I've never been good with traffic, and the freeway was an absolutely parking lot.

The bus driver, "It was a pleasure chauffeuring you ladies today," as he extended his hand to assist each of us off the bus, "Watch your step."

Not one person responded when Shay said, (and quite loudly). "I don't know why we're tipping him anyway, he's getting paid already, so why are we giving him more money, he just did his job."

As though he didn't hear Shay, the driver said, "I enjoyed the conversations, laughs and songs, and thank you also for the concert ticket as well. I enjoyed it. I look forward to rolling with you again."

Evette said, "Thanks for letting us sisters roll."

He laughed.

The security guard at the church looked as though he was very happy to see us all return so he could lock up the parking lot and go home. We went around and hugged one another when someone said, "Group hug."

As we separated from our group hug we saw two men walking towards us. As Gramby would say, "We don't see their kind in this neighborhood often."

I didn't see their car on the lot when we pulled up, but more than likely I was busy running my mouth. As they walked up I also noticed two females exiting another vehicle. I've always paid attention to license plates and that was no different this night, I looked at the license plate of the car the two men were in and noticed it was an "EXEMPT" plate. Hmmm, official business. Surely they didn't stop by the church to see what time Sunday service starts, but why were they here? I wondered.

The church security guard approached them, and asked, "May I help you?"

"Good evening," as they perused all the ladies still gathered around the bus. "We're looking for Ms. Shay McGlover."

I said, "Shay McGlover? What do you want with Shay?"

"Where is she? Which one of you ladies is Shay?" As they continued to look around the large crowd of ladies still standing around the bus.

I said nothing else. I won't lie, for a second I wished I said, "She's not here."

One of the gentlemen walked over to Shay and asked, "Are you Shay McGlover?"

With an attitude Shay asked, "Who's asking?"

He handed her a business card of which no one else could see.

She looked up and said, "And?"

"And, are you Shay McGlover?"

"According to your card you're the investigator, so you figure out if I'm Shay McGlover or not."

At that time a female stepped closer to them, and opened a folder, from my vantage point the photo she showed the gentleman was surely Shay. All the ladies standing around looked on with concern.

I asked, "What's going on Sir?"

Reaching behind, he came forward with a pair of handcuffs. Some ladies reacted with loud gasps of shock and put their hands over their mouths. My instinct was to grab for my cousin. Not realizing both my hands were on this man's arm, I said, "Sir, what's going on? You have the wrong person. This is my cousin and we were all at dinner and a concert tonight, you must have the wrong person because she didn't do anything. I swear we've been together all day today."

He looked down towards his arm, and that was my cue that I needed to let his arm go.

"Oh, I'm sorry, but honestly you must have the wrong person."

Others pleaded, "Sir, she's been with us all night."

The female officer came over and searched Shay; as she wiggled a bit, "Don't touch me."

"Can someone tell me what's going on? Where are you taking her? Shay you can leave your purse with me?"

"No, her purse and car are going with us."

Finally one of the gentlemen handed me his card. I looked down at the card and said. "What the heck is going on here?"

"Investigator Israel Salle, Federal Bureau of Investigation."

"Shay what's going on?"

"I don't know, ask them. They're just gonna show up here for no reason; ask them, they seem to know everything. All these women here and they single me out for no reason."

"And we do know everything, Ms. Shay McGlover you're under arrest." The female officer read off her rights, and I've watched enough television to know when a cop is telling you, "You have the right to remain silent," and so forth, you're probably not sleeping in your own bed that night.

"Shay what's going on?"

She turned her head.

"What do you need me to do?"

"I keep telling you, I don't need anyone to do anything for me. Go on with your little girls in my circle group. I'll be fine, I don't know what this is about, nor do I know why they showed up at the church like this."

The officers led Shay to their vehicle.

"Sir, can you tell me what's going on?"

Toya turned to me and said, "Come on Brooklyn, you're obviously not going to get any information tonight, let's get you home."

"It's late now, we have to question Ms. McGlover tonight or in the morning, I would suggest you call me tomorrow and I can at least give you her location, that's the best I can do tonight. You ladies have a good evening."

We all watched as they put Shay into the backseat of their car, "Watch your head ma'am."

Shay had no expression as they put her in the car, quite honestly she looked the same as she had on the bus ride, unfazed, unconcerned. I know with great certainty if a cop put handcuffs on me and put me in the backseat of the car I would at least shed a tear or two, or protest or something, not Shay. She seemed cool as a cucumber.

"Wow, that's some heck of a way to end a birthday celebration isn't it? Somehow it always winds up being about Shay, huh?"

"Let's go Brook."

As exhausted as I was from the birthday events I couldn't sleep at all, and this time it wasn't due to hot flashes. It wasn't that I slept too long the previous night and couldn't sleep now; it wasn't any of the usual insomnia things. This time I was concerned about Shay. How in the world had she wound up in jail? Deep down inside I felt it was all some mistake and it would be resolved the next day, I figured come the wee hours of the morning I would get a call from her asking me to pick her up. Regardless of the fact that she never needs anyone, I'd go get her.

Perhaps her nonchalant, non-caring attitude was indication that she too knew she hadn't done anything and knew it would be ironed out swiftly upon getting to the station. Maybe that's why my reaction and the reactions of all the other ladies far exceeded Shay's, she didn't display any worry because she had nothing to worry about. Yeah that's it. One thing I knew with great certainty was that my cousin was too smart to give up her freedom. I kept trying to figure it out; this has to be some type of mistaken identity type thing. I sat on my bed trying to figure it all out, she's educated, she's got a good job, yeah she has an attitude, but she's not a criminal. I tried to focus on something Gramby always said, "If you're going to pray, don't worry; and if you're going to worry, don't pray."

I rested in that and fell asleep...finally.

I couldn't wait til' 10:00 a.m., I called the investigator and he didn't give me much information, pretty much told me that the courts are an open forum and that Shay would be going to court in two days.

"Two days?"

"That girl will nut up in jail for two days, and I probably will too, worrying about her."

He gave me the court and division information and also told me where Shay was housed. I didn't like that word too much; it was a term that put me in the frame of mind that someone would be staying a while.

Shay hadn't as much called me when she received her phone calls; I wondered if she'd called her mother. I didn't want to be the one to upset her mother, to be honest I was praying everything would be ironed out before she knew anything about it.

Before ending our call, the investigator said, "I would advise you to wait until after the court date to visit her, she'll be processed in by then, but she does get phone calls, so perhaps she'll call you."

"Well she hasn't called yet. And, you called out a lot of charges when you were at the church that night arresting Shay, can you tell me what they are?"

"You'll be able to hear everything in court."

The conversation ended with me not knowing any more than I did before the call, well, except the court date. I tried my best to remember the codes the officers spewed out as they arrested her, but I couldn't remember. If I could remember I could do a little research myself. Of course it wouldn't tell me everything, but it would tell me something.

Each time the phone rang I nearly broke my neck to answer it. This was a first for me, never in my life had I wished for a collect call from a jail before. Honestly I couldn't even remember the last time I anxiously awaited a call from Shay. Truth be told, the negativity was such that I'd gotten to where I didn't care if she called or not.

Curiosity got the best of me; I called the jail and obtained her bail amount. My God, I wasn't expecting that at all. I kept repeating, what in the world have you done Shay? As though she could hear me, I repeated it over and over again. I tried to distract myself with the thought she made this bed, she has to lie in it, but that didn't work for me either. It didn't make me feel the least bit better. I tried to make a conscious effort not to let it drive me crazy for two days, but that was easier said than done.

I sat down on the floor in the den and opened up all the gifts the ladies had given me, and read some of the notes they wrote on my friendship cards. I opened Jourdain's card to find three hundred dollars in it. I grinned. I guess she didn't forget after all. And, of course it would take Evette to make me crack up in the midst of so much going on with Shay. She wrote, *Friends are like underwear, some snap under pressure; some don't have the strength to hold you up; some get a little bit twisted, and some really do cover your butt when you need them to.*

Thanks Evette, I needed that.

The court date seemed to take forever, there was Shay dressed like all the other inmates. I'm sure she hated that. She looked just as nonchalant and unconcerned as she did the night they arrested her, often appearing to just be a spectator when listening to other cases and not an inmate herself. She laughed at other cases, obviously judging others on something stupid they'd done, yet there she was seated right there next to them. One inmate's case was about him taking checks out of the back of someone's checkbook, thinking the person wouldn't notice the money was gone until they got to that particular number in their check book. Knowing Shay she was thinking to herself, *he can't be that dumb.*

All of my efforts to get Shay's attention were met with negative results, and I believe she did it on purpose; she didn't want to look at me. I pictured her to be embarrassed but trying not to act as though she was.

Everything went so fast. Defendant after defendant took their brief time before the judge, and Shay was no different.

"The next case is Shay McGlover, will you please stand."

Shay took her time standing up as though the judge had all the time in the world. Your charges are as follows, just as the detective had did the night she was arrested the judge quickly spewed out penal codes, the only one I caught was PC487.

"Ms. McGlover how do you plea?"

"What?"

"I said how do you plea, and you might want to tame that attitude of yours. Again, how do you plea?"

Shay barked back, "Not guilty what else?"

After giving Shay her next court date, four weeks away, the judge moved on to the next case, "Ward Walker, please stand."

Interrupting the judge, Shay hollered, "How long do you guys plan to keep me in here?"

The officers removed Shay from the courtroom, not once did she look back to see if anyone was there for her, though I really do think she saw me, but avoided eye contact. I couldn't believe I sat there for three hours for her to have three minutes, if that, before the judge.

"Good morning, I was in court this morning and things went so fast I don't have any more information than I did before today. I couldn't write down all the charges fast enough, and I'd also like to know if they have reduced her bail? I feel like I'm going stir crazy worrying about my cousin."

He seemed to have a softer demeanor than the day of the arrest.

"Good Morning Miss, I'm sorry, your last name escapes me, but do you mind if I call you Brooklyn?"

"No, problem, that's fine. Brooklyn it is."

"Thanks. First let me say it's not likely that the bail will be reduced, and let me say Ms. McGlover is in a lot of hot water. Her next court date is in four weeks."

"Four weeks? You've got to be kidding. She has to stay there for four more weeks?"

"Yes, unless she's bailed out. I have no doubt she'll be incarcerated for a lot longer than four weeks, but of course there is a court process we have to go through. You know there's always the option of her being bailed out. But, that's a decision her family needs to make."

"Well, her family doesn't have that type of money that's for sure."

"You know, if I were you I would relax and allow things to run its course. At this point there's not a lot you can do anyway. On a more personal note I recently went through this with a family member, and we had to come to terms with the fact that sometimes our hands are tied, and there's nothing we can do, and quite honestly I think that's where you are. Shay's put herself in a real pickle. I would suggest you visit her and get more information, as we continue to work on our case. She's not talking much to us, but that's okay, we have enough videos and computer information to seal our case, oh and witness testimony of course. Again, let the process take its course. Sometimes we bail people out of things so much in life, until finally they get involved in something where no one can help them. But, also sometimes it's good to let folks stew in their own pots sometimes, they sometimes learn more than when someone is always running to the rescue."

"I hear you. I'm having trouble believing all of this."

"I understand."

"Investigator, I'm wondering if you're sure you have the right person, because my cousin isn't stupid enough to land herself in jail, we love our freedom too much. Yeah she's got an attitude, and yeah, she's a bit on the uppity side, but a criminal? No Sir."

"Yeah, well we wouldn't have made an arrest if we didn't have sufficient evidence to do so. You can't steal money from people and get away with it. Your cousin got greedy; had she stopped a few years ago it's possible no one would have ever noticed, but she got comfortable and greedy."

"What!!! Stealing money? No way. We were raised to work hard for whatever we get. Are you sure about this?"

"Yes Brooklyn, I'm sure. And, she may not have been a criminal at some point in her life, but she is now."

"Man, I'm sorry, I'm having trouble believing you."

"Oh I understand, it's natural for family and other loved ones to feel that way and run to the defense of their family member when they don't have all the details. They've known this person all their life, and can't fathom they'd do these things. It happens all the time. Have you seen the mothers on the news sometimes hollering into the television screen that their son is not a murderer? The most recent case was that one on Western Avenue, do you remember that one?"

I held the phone in silence, he continued, "If you recall the mother responded to the scene hollering, "My son does not have a gun!!! They are lying, they planted it," but after all the videos from neighboring businesses were turned over to the police what did they see? Her son with a gun in his hand. Now don't get me wrong Brooklyn, we don't get it right all the time, and I'll admit that some in my profession have made this job a bit difficult for others with things they've done, but again, while we don't get it right all the time, I can tell you with great certainty that this isn't one of those times where we didn't get it right. I don't know your cousin, so I have nothing to gauge anything by, but somewhere she had a lapse in judgment. Can I ask you something?"

"Sure."

"How'd you think Shay was living the lifestyle she was living?"

Before I answered his question I thought of all the times Shay criticized others, often making very nasty statements about someone's dress being cheap, or purses being a knock off, or "I can't believe she's still driving that same car." I thought about all the statements made judging others, and all the times she made comments to me about how I needed to live more, "When you see something you want just get it, you only live once." I thought about the day I asked Shay what money tree she had found to be able to shop so much all the time. My mind went to the times she was critical of me for the places I liked to shop and dine at, calling them too low budget. I remembered the times Shay would buy expensive bottles of perfumes, and hand me one as though it was nothing to hand someone a $400 bottle of perfume. I thought about all the times she told me to forget about sticking to a budget, "You can't take any of that money with you, spend it." And, last but not least I thought about the time she liked two cars and decided to just buy them both.

"Brooklyn, did you hear my question? How'd you think Shay was living the lifestyle she was living?"

I stuttered, "She works every day; she has a pretty decent job. Plus her dad left her some money."

"We've covered all of our bases, and we checked into that as well. He only left her $10,000, the rest went to her two brothers due to some discord in the family, and that's been gone. You never questioned the type of cars she drives, where she lives, or her overall lifestyle?"

"I really felt it was money her father left her, working every day, proper budgeting, and to be honest I wasn't around Shay that much, I'd put some distance between us. Shay can be pretty hard to be around sometimes."

"Well that's a good thing, no need in you being involved in any of this."

"Let me ask you something else."

"Yes Sir?"

"Were you aware of all the Go Fund Me accounts she had going?"

"Go Fund Me accounts?"

"Yes. She's never mentioned those to you?"

"Well, we've talked about them in general conversation before about how others shouldn't be creating these accounts for illegitimate reasons, and how it's abusing the kindness of others. I don't know if you saw the lady on television last month who was arrested for defrauding a bunch of people saying she had cancer, she cut all her hair off and everything, and had never been diagnosed with cancer. Those are the types of things Shay and I would talk about."

"And, I'm sorry to tell you, but those are the very things Shay has been doing, coming up with tear-jerking, gut wrenching stories to pull on the heart strings of people to donate to her cause. She's had at least four deceased husband's funeral's funded."

"I can't believe this…wow. Well she's only had two husbands. Shay, Shay, Shay, what were you thinking?"

"She's also been taking money from many unassuming customers at the bank. She started off with small withdrawals a few years ago, we assume those funded her food and gas for the week, but then like I said she got greedy and took larger amounts and people started coming forward. To be perfectly honest with you I don't think these individuals should have been doing banking by themselves anyway, I feel due to their frailty and age they should have been accompanied by a family member, but that's neither here nor there, they should be able to go to the bank and do their banking without being ripped off by a bank employee."

"True."

"I think she counted the money out so fast to these elderly folks until they didn't catch on that they never left the bank with the correct amount in the first place. Her undoing was putting her name on a couple of accounts and beneficiary cards, of course family members would question that when someone passed on, and that's where we were called to get involved."

"I'm speechless. Wow, this is a mess. This kind of explains some things."

"What do you mean?"

"How she was able to not ever worry about money, it seems where everyone else was budgeting she never seemed to have to. But I'll be honest, I know you're telling me all of this, but I'll have to sit through the proceedings to hear the evidence before I truly believe it, because I can't believe she'd be that stupid."

"You're more than welcome to."

"Man, Shay…this is a mess."

"That's an understatement."

"I assume she'll get jail time?"

"Yeah, I think we can definitely count on jail time. How much, I don't know. She's not very cooperative, so I don't see her taking a plea deal, but that would probably be to her benefit."

"Well I guess our grandmother was right."

"Right about what?"

"She always said, "Life is simple, we're the ones who complicate it.""

"Yes, Shay has definitely complicated her life. Well Brooklyn, I think that's about it for now, if you have any other questions feel free to call me."

I made my way to the federal jail to visit Shay. It was something about that word "federal" on the building out front that made me feel some type of way, for some reason it made me feel a bit more uneasy than if it said county jail. Why? I don't know. I don't want to ever be in either jail, but every time I'd ever heard the word "federal," the nickname of "the big boys" followed.

I stood in line for a couple of hours with everyone else waiting for visiting hours to start, in the excruciating outdoor heat. I must've looked at the signs around the visiting area a hundred times while waiting FEDERAL DETENTION CENTER. Really Shay?

She came out looking just as nonchalant as she always did, I spoke, "Hi."

She grunted, "Hi."

"I've been down here three times and they told me you wouldn't come out for your visit."

"And?"

"And what?"

"Why would you have me come down here and not come out like that? I've stood out there at least two hours each time."

"I didn't have you come down anywhere; you came on your own. I didn't come out for my visit because I didn't want to, you ever think of that?"

"Really Shay?"

"Shay what's going on? Do you know you have a pretty hefty bail?"

"Yeah. Can you pay it?"

"No, so what are you worrying about it for, you can't help me?"

"Do you have money in the bank to bail yourself out?"

"They froze my accounts. What do you want Brooklyn?"

"So you can't lose the attitude even in this situation?"

"Why do you care Brooklyn, I don't. You can leave now."

I grabbed my purse and turned to walk out. "I'm here because you're my cousin Shay. They say you took money from the bank and bank customers, and something about a bunch of fraudulent Go Fund Me accounts, is it true Shay? Did you do it?"

"They're the detectives, let them figure it out."

"Well that's a crazy answer. Either you did or you didn't do it?"

"Whatever...like I said you can go now."

Without saying another word, and with much time left on the visitation clock, Shay got up, walked away from the window, and never looked back.

Though she couldn't hear me I said, "That's the last time you'll leave me at a visitation window."

I walked back to the car and so many things became so clear.

Tracy Brooks

A good friend knows all your best stories; a best friend has lived them with you.

Some friends come into your life for a reason; others come only for a season.

Some people come into our lives for a reason, some are a blessing, some are a lesson.

There are good ships and wood ships, ships that sail the sea; but the best ships are friendships may they always be.

Life is not always about what happens to us, but, how we handle it.

Hatred corrodes the vessel in which it is stored.

EPILOGUE

Shay

Like many others held up in this hell hole of a prison, I wasn't sorry for anything. I guess it's like when I got caught as a child with my hand in Gramby's cookie jar, I wasn't sorry I took the cookie. I wanted the cookie. I was only sorry I got caught, and that's how I felt when I first got here. No doubt but for being arrested I would still be doing the same thing, taking people's money without permission. Nice people, people who trusted me. People who put money in envelopes for me at Christmas time, and when and if they found out it was my birthday, they did the same. Yet I violated their trust, felt entitled to someone else's money. No valid reason for my actions, I had a great job, great pay, I guess it can be summed up to one word: Greed. It wasn't as though I lacked anything, or as though I was missing any meals, it was plain and simple: Greed, along with just not giving a darn.

Even with that I still sit here sometimes with this attitude of entitlement, this attitude of blaming others. Truth be told I didn't take anything serious until the verdict was read. Quite honestly, I expected I'd get a little slap on the wrist similar to what I'd seen others get for doing far more than I'd ever done.

Often I heard Gramby's voice so clear I thought she was locked up with me. Though there's never a quiet moment in this place, always a cell door slamming, an intercom paging someone, someone hollering just to be hollering, I could still hear Gramby's voice crystal clear drowning out all other sounds.

"When you know better you do better."

I mumble that aloud from time to time, *when you know better you do better*. Surely I knew better. It often felt as though I was chastising myself each time I said it.

Deliberate efforts would be made to stop thinking of Gramby and all her little sayings, only to hear things even louder, *"Honey chile, people don't get away with anything in this life, they just haven't got caught yet."*

Or, one of her all-time favorites when all the grandchildren would run into the house telling her what some other neighborhood kids did, and what their parents allowed them to do, and where their parents allowed them to go and there we were pleading our case to do the same.

"Well, let me tell you this, I'm not raising those kids, I'm raising you, and you can't do what they do. You can't do what other people do, because you just might not get the outcome others get."

Well ain't that the truth. All the times I've heard of folks on the news or from my old neighborhood getting a slap on the wrist, yet I got time. What happened to first time offenders getting a break? Every time Ms. Cunningham's son got arrested I would look up the next week and there he was back on the front porch again, up to no good. He'd come across the street to my house to have my mother pray for him before each court date, asking her to pray that his court case went in his favor. And, sure enough it would. I still don't know if that was the right thing to do, for her to be praying for him to get off instead of his just desserts, but look at me now wishing I got that slap on the wrist too. It seemed the most time he was ever given was thirty days, if that.

My anger for the judge handling my case hasn't diminished much. I often still get fuming mad at how he so easily slammed his little gavel down causing some people to jump, including me, after he sentenced me to four years.

"Four years!!! Are you kidding me?! I can't do four years!!! Are you serious?!"

Before I could finish my last sentence of protest, two burly deputies were just about lifting me off of my feet carting me out of the courtroom. All I could hear was the judge calling for the next case on the calendar to come forth.

My attorney told me that if I had lost some of my attitude during the proceedings, showed some type of remorse, lost some of that arrogance, that just maybe I would have been given probation, community service or at the very least a shorter sentence. But no, I was still in my I don't care about anything tough girl attitude.

It all reminded me of Gramby's word, "Life is simple, we're the ones who complicate it. If you look over your life you'll find the one person that caused you more pain and strife than anyone else, and who disappointed you the most, you'll find it's the person in the mirror."

The same attitude I had been lugging around with me the last six years I brought to the court, and then to the prison with me. I didn't want to talk to anyone, and still carried that better than you attitude. They all deserved to be here, not me. They're criminals, not me. They grew up on the other side of the tracks, not me.

In a short time I was able to see who the loud mouths in the bunch were in my pod. I was able to decipher who needed attention, who thought she was bigger and better than everyone else, who thought she was all that and a bag of chips, who had to have the last word in everything, who the mess starter was, always starting rumors and tension in the pod; who had nothing good to say about anyone else, and whose conversation was always about them. If their mouths were moving they were talking about them self.

I listened to all of the conversations of how many of the women described prison for them as a "revolving door." I was amazed at how some seemed happy to be back, calling it "three hots and a cot."

Some had conversations of what they would do differently not to get caught the next time. But for me, I didn't see a next time coming. Lesson learned. Living somewhere where you're told when to wake up, eat, shower and use the bathroom is not for me.

It was very hard to be around most of these females but I had no choice. It wasn't as though it was some exclusive hotel where I could request a special suite just for me, or a room change. It wasn't a hotel, it was prison.

Recently while sitting on yet another hard bench watching and listening to everyone in my pod, I drifted off very quickly in my mind. The words came from out of nowhere because I had absolutely nothing on my mind at that particular time. The words were, *You don't like them because they're just like you.* I tried to shake it off a bit, distract the thought, think about something else, but again, *they're just like you.* It hit me like a bolt of lightning, and the mere thought was hurtful. Was I as obnoxious, self-centered, and rude as these females were? I tried hard to deny it, but it was true. Yes I was.

Somewhere along this journey I'd become that female I didn't like myself. Self-absorbed, mean, arrogant, unappreciative, cantankerous, judgmental, entitled, selfish, demeaning, yes, I'd become one who lacked compassion for others. Wow, I'd become entitled, rude, jealous. I stopped there with my thoughts though I felt many other words could describe me very well, but that was all I could handle at the time. *You've become the type of female you never liked being around yourself.* Yeah that's exactly what happened. I allowed life to make me bitter instead of better. I lost my COMEBACK!! Gramby used to always talk about us never losing our comeback. But, at some point it's obvious that I took my gloves off and let everything hit me and knock me down without swinging anymore, I lost my fight. Defeated! Got pissed off over a few things, and decided to stay mad. Folks had been mean to me and I decided to become that mean person, too. People had walked over me and my feelings, and I decided that's the way I was going to be also, it seemed to be working for them. I decided nice wasn't working for me anymore, so I'd be as mean as others had been to me. I won't care about anyone or anything either.

As Dr. Phil would say, "Well, how'd that work out for you?"

Well obviously it was all to my detriment, because I'm the one now looking at life through bars.

"*You can't do everything everyone else does.*"

Okay Gramby, I hear you!

Most of my tick off came from relationships, but then as I sat on the bench I thought of something Gramby said. *If you keep falling for the same type of men you're going to get the same results. Quit dating the same man.*

"Huh?"

"You're dating the same man."

"No I'm not."

"Yes you are, you get the same type of man, he just has a different name."

"Oh."

"Stop Building A Bear!"

"Gramby, what are you talking about?"

"You've never heard that before?"

"No ma'am."

"Well in your case it's when you keep meeting these guys who come to you broken over everything from finances, child support issues, divorce, and the list goes on, and you think he's such a good guy you try to make him feel better about himself, and you help build him up…building a bear. You help him snap on his confidence again, you help him snap on some self-esteem, he gets his swag back, his chest starts sticking out, he's walking straighter, before long he's feeling so much better about himself that he snaps on some shoes and walks right off. He only needed you when life was low. Stop building a bear."

Sitting there allowing the thoughts to replay in my mind I started to tear up. *You've become that female you don't like.* Each time I thought of words of wisdom from both my mother and Gramby I just about lost it, but would hurriedly divert my attention elsewhere in the pod to not allow others to see me crack. Somehow because I wouldn't socialize with others in my pod I was giving the nickname Hard Hannah. Some days the bullies in the pod would try to provoke me with words to get me to talk and they too were ignored.

"Oh Hard Hannah thinks she's better than everyone else."

"Does she talk? What, are you too good to talk to us? Honey you're locked up just like us, so you're not any better than us? You have a prison number just like us girlfriend."

I'd look at them, and not say a word. I'm not one who knows much about the street life, never lived it, but what I do know is that bullies talk and talk and *talk*, and generally that's all they're going to do is talk! So their words meant nothing to me. Often when it's time for a fight to begin the bully is the first one running, because they're only weapon is words.

I tried to blink and get myself together, but the same thoughts kept coming to my mind. *You've become that female you don't like.* Different questions kept barging into my mind: How do you expect others to like you when you don't like yourself? What happened to the Shay who could turn lemons to lemonade? Or better yet, limes to margaritas. What happened to the Shay who could always see the bright side of any situation? The one who always saw the cup half full, instead of half empty. How'd I become so bitter? Where's that Shay who helped others all the time, that Shay who would encouraged others to not let life beat them down?

I thought about all the packages that came for me all the time. They were addressed from Brooklyn, my mother, and of course Girls In My Circle. I'd receive the boxes from the guards and toss them in a corner somewhere because I was still holding on to that nasty I don't need anyone attitude. I don't want their packages, I don't need anyone. I thought about the day another female approached me.

"You must have a large family and a lot of friends, you get mail and packages every week."

I shrugged my shoulders like it was nothing, because that's what it was to me, nothing.

"I've been here three years and haven't received as much as a letter from anyone. I think my family has worn tired of me going through this revolving door. I've been so ungrateful they're allowing me to figure life out for myself now. You know when you go to prison you kind of drag everyone with you. If your family isn't lining up to visit you, they're taking time to write you and send you things, but in my case it's an emotional prison for my family, and I think they are tired of it all. The crazy thing is I know better, I just don't do better."

Wow, I've heard those words before. *I hear you Gramby.*

"I can't believe you never open anything. You don't want it?"

"No you can have it."

I watched as a few ladies tore through the boxes as though someone had just dropped off a million dollars, only to have Lynelle approach me later, "Here, I saved some of the toiletries for you, and I've been holding these letters for you until you're ready to read them, don't throw them out. People are going out of their way to make sure you know you're loved and not forgotten about, don't just throw these things out. There are people in here who wish they had loved ones to send them something. Re-think this; people are spending their time and money to make sure you know they love you. I kept some of the inspirational books, you might want to flip through them one day too, they've helped me."

Still in my attitude, I moaned out a sorry little, "Thank you."

Lynelle didn't know it, but she was somehow helping to break down my hardness, each time I talked to her I felt my attitude chipping away.

She was the quiet one in the bunch, but she was surely a bright light. She didn't handle a domestic abuse situation the way the court system thought it should be handled, and therefore found herself here for three years.

Lynelle said, "I sometimes wonder if the situation could have been handled differently."

"Well, at least you're here to talk about it, you could have been killed."

She made me think that I too could have handled my own life differently. She wore her quietness differently than me, if that makes any sense. Mine came off as a bad attitude of one totally angry and mad at the world, but hers came off as meekness. She had a very beautiful humbleness about her. She made me wonder why I had hid the light I used to carry. She made me think of Dr. King's comment about light and darkness. *Only light can drive out darkness*. Most of all, she made me wonder how I became that female I didn't like. Our short conversations made me want to come out of all this darkness. Our conversations made me question myself, how'd you become that person who can say any and everything you want to say to someone, but when the script is flipped you have the nerves to have an attitude? She made me remember something I heard Reverend Clark say before, "Oh you have 20/20 vision when looking at everyone else, but you can't see when it comes to the things you need to change about yourself. Oh you're blind as a bat then."

Often when Lynelle left my immediate area I got to where I anxiously awaited the next time we sat down and talked. It made me think of Gramby, "You know the Lord always sends someone. You might not listen to me now, or get the whole message when it comes from me, but someone else might come along one day and pretty much say the same thing, just a wee bit differently, and you'll finally get it."

It was easy to be around Lynelle, she was positive and not always complaining. She made me have some ahh haa moments. *Yeah, that's why my friends no longer come around; they get tired of all the complaining.* She had this welcoming spirit that made me feel comfortable talking to her, and better yet, a spirit that made me listen to her. I felt an approach of genuine love. Oh I know everything my family has told me has also been in love, but I guess it's kind of like a smoker, or addict, you hear it when you're ready to hear it. Plus, unlike times when others told me something about my attitude and behavior where I had the ability to walk off, slam the door, drive off and leave, that wasn't quite the case here. Lynelle's conversations came off more as advice, rather than feeling as though I was being chastised.

She always pointed things out to me, "You see all that going on over there in the pod, you never want to be seen treating people like that, and you never want to be that person who doesn't care about the next person."

I was able to see so much now as I watched others, but couldn't see it in myself until now. I couldn't believe I'd become *that person.*

I watched as females in the pod said some of the meanest things to one another. I watched as many couldn't even speak to one another. I saw such hatred and again I thought, *you'd become that person.* Where did I change? I remembered how Pastor Clark once said, "Have you noticed the energy it takes to make sure you walk in this direction not to have to speak to this person, and go this way not to have to run into that person, and how you try to turn your head and act like you don't see this person, and all the effort it takes not to speak? JUST SPEAK!! Say, "Good Morning. It's simple, why complicate it?"

One day I stood up for someone in the prison when ladies were belittling and talking down to her, "You don't have to stand there and let people talk to you that way, come over here with us."

That's something the old Shay would have done, but how embarrassing it was to remember not too long ago being that person on the other end spewing mean words out.

"You know sometimes when you stand back and watch something from a different angle you can see things more clearly."

Okay, I hear you Gramby.

Well, that's exactly what happened. I saw myself in many of these interactions, and unfortunately I was seeing the type of person I'd been to others, always trying to cut someone with my tongue, dead set on making others hurt like I hurt for so many years. Yeah, I guess it's true, hurt people hurt people. I spoke audibly, but no one was close enough to hear my soft words to myself. *You became the person no one liked to be around. You're the one no one wants to invite because of the aura you lug around. You're the one people hated to see coming.*

I was at a point where I wished the words in my head would shut off. But then the word Diversion came to mind. *Yep, Always verbally beating people up, always criticizing others, always talking about others as a way of diverting the attention from myself and what I was doing. Put the spotlight on others to take it off of me. Yes, I'd become the person I didn't like.*

The mere thought of it all gave me a good whoopin'. Did I have to be stopped and set still to see things clearly? Did the judge do me a favor? Whew, I have a hard time admitting that one, but perhaps it's true. How low would I have gone if I hadn't been stopped? I continued to think about the Go Fund Me accounts. Really Shay? You stooped that low to hash up stories that you knew would tug at the hearts of others for the almighty dollar. Are you serious? It really is the root of all evil. I used to talk about those type of people myself, building pages asking for money to bury a loved one who died five years ago. Really? *You became that person.*

My mind was going a hundred miles a minute. *Wow, you really did become the person you didn't like. You belittled people over their income sometimes, yet much of the money you had wasn't even yours.*

I thought on the days when someone sent a pleasant "Good Morning" my way, and all I could say was, "What's so good about it?"

Tears filled my eyes when I thought about how Brooklyn got so mad at me and just about tore me in two, "What do you mean what's so good about it? You woke up this morning didn't you? You have family, you have a job, you have food on the table, you have clothes, I see some shoes on your feet, and the last I checked you aren't laying up in some hospital, should I go on?"

"No you can stop there."

I thought about the promotions I put in for and didn't get, and how mad I was that I didn't get the job. Yet, I never once focused on the fact that the promotional jobs I applied for were cut in the budget within two years, so that could have been me headed to the unemployment line. But it wasn't.

Quite honestly I was now embarrassed by my actions. I thought about all the days I had to comment on everything and everyone. All others present saw the same things I did, but said nothing.

"She couldn't put on anything better than that?" I said to Brooklyn one day.

"Maybe that's all she has Shay, but you have a closet full of clothes maybe you can give her a few pieces."

Or, the time Brooklyn gently asked the waitress if she could move our seat. Honestly that should have been the end of it, and the situation considered resolved. But, no, I had to turn around to the mother of this child and say, "Maybe you should keep him home if he doesn't know how to act in a restaurant. He's disrupting the whole restaurant!"

Brooklyn grabbed my arm, "Shay!!! Stop it!!! You see he has some medical problem!"

"Yeah, but his problem isn't my problem. I came out to relax and enjoy myself."

No wonder Brooklyn stopped going places with me. The last time we went out together I believe I really broke the camel's back and she was done. It took everything I had for her not to grab Uber to take her home. After what I said to Mrs. Griffin, and then the lady in the parking lot, I think Brooklyn had had it.

"Look at her parking there she knows she's not handicapped."

Again, Brooklyn grabbed my arm, "Something is going to happen to you out here, and it's not funny Shay, you can get us both hurt."

"She's walking pretty good to me."

As we got into my car the lady hollered, "Excuse me, I forgot to send you the memo that I was diagnosed with multiple sclerosis last year. Did you know you can't see all handicaps from the outside sometimes."

Brooklyn apologized to the lady, as she often did on my behalf.

Lynelle walked over when I was thinking of something I said to Michee at Brooklyn's party about her husband who has PTSD. I totally lacked compassion and my skinned crawled at the words I said to her that night. Wow, I can't believe I said that. My mind shifted to a lady at work who was always taking off sick, but because she always looked well and dressed nice I made comments that she was playing the system, and then I was too mean to apologize for that when she came in months later with no hair from chemo. Why'd I make everyone else's business my business? Oh, to divert the attention off myself; to make myself look better by demeaning others. How'd I get to where the only opinion that counted was mine, and the only person who mattered was me?

Lynelle asked, "What's wrong?"

"Oh, I'm just going over some things in my mind that I've done and said to people, and it's not a pretty picture. I feel I owe a bunch of people apologies."

"Well first start with forgiving yourself, you'll find that's the toughest one to get."

"Yeah, I think you're right there."

I told Lynelle about some of the things that were whirling through my mind, including the times Brooklyn would chastise me about handicap spots, "You can't park there anyway Shay, why are you worried about it?" Or, the times I would go up to someone and ask, "Why would a female as pretty as you tattoo your face like that?"

I told Lynelle how Brooklyn would grab my arm and tell me that I can't just walk up to any and every one I chose to , and how she always said, "Someone's going to punch you in your mouth one day."

But sitting here going down memory lane, I'm wondering if a punch in the mouth would have been easier, at least I would have healed from that by now, because it's the inner scars I'm dealing with now.

Lynelle cut my trip down memory lane short by saying, "Hear me, and hear me good, I've come to learn that *the best apology is changed behavior.*"

With a smirk on my face, and a tight hug from Lynelle, I said, "You know what, that's exactly what I plan to do. I'm going to remember that."

I repeated what she said, the best apology is changed behavior, the best apology is changed behavior.

Lynelle reminded me of the day we first met. "Oh you were tough, wouldn't let anyone get too close to you, I remember when I asked you your name and you barked some numbers at me."

"My name is #PF38493."

"And I had to tell you to never let anyone reduce your name down to just another number."

"Yeah I remember."

Lynelle handed me a stack of letters she'd been grabbing for me out of the boxes that Shay and her friends sent.

"I think you need to open and read some of these. It looks like you have a bunch of people who love you. Read them."

Reading the letters was tough. I hadn't opened them thinking they'd be full of mean spirited words within, venom like I would spew out, but instead they were all filled with encouragement. Brooklyn also included a few letters from my mom and kids, and that brought tears to my eyes. I'd been so negative to be around even my kids had distanced themselves. I was in awe of the strength of love in the letters and cards. While reading one I thought about a story my dad used to tell me when I was little about how a master could have a hundred sheep, yet one can get lost and he'll leave those ninety-nine that he knows are okay, to find that one. In reading the letters engulf with love I pictured that I was that one lost sheep everyone was trying to reel back in.

I sat down at a table and started returning some of the letters. I didn't disclose in any of the letters how I'd been working on myself and going to bible studies, and different classes to help change my ways. If any of the ladies were the least bit like me they would have the usual cynical comment people make when they hear someone locked up is going to church and bible study, "Well what else is it for them to do in there, the real test will be how they act when they're released."

And, like Lynelle said, *the best apology is changed behavior*, and I figured I could show them, better than telling them.

Lynelle, "Come go to the church service with me."

"No, not this time, I wanted to finish writing my letters."

"Girl please, you've ignored all these letters all of this time, you can get back to them in about an hour. Plus I put your name on the list for those wishing to attend the service."

"Okay."

The visiting minister had a display with him to make his point for his sermon. It was a picture of the mall directory kiosk that depicts a RED DOT showing you exactly where you are.

He pointed to the display, and continued to close out his sermon, "You go to this RED DOT to find out how to get where you're trying to go. You don't plan to just stand at the RED DOT. So let's take a minute for you to picture this RED DOT as where you are in your life right now; think about whatever decisions, choices, paths you took to get you to this RED DOT. Again, generally no one stays at the RED DOT; it's a place you go to see where you are to get where you're going. My question to you is, do you plan to stay at this RED DOT or do you plan to use this location as a starting point to get where you really need to go in life? And I'm sure it's not this prison right?"

I responded as if he was only speaking to me, "Right."

I don't think I've had that much fun ever in my life. It's amazing the fun you can have when you drop the attitude. I sang and participated with all the songs and games, instead of acting as though I was above it all, or instead of acting like whatever they were doing was childish.

A month after my release Brooklyn invited me to her women's fellowship trip. In the past that was something I would normally decline, but instead I hopped on the bus with fifty nine other women. I was a little hesitant at first because I felt I would be bombarded with questions about the last four years of my life, or treated like an outcast. To the contrary, unlike me and how I may have held on to some things if the roles were reversed, they all welcomed me with opened arms. The only mention of prison life was when the food was being passed around the bus and I got ahold of Brooklyn's potato salad. I loved her potato salad, not too sweet, not too sour, just perfect. It was then I made the one and only comment that was made.

"It sure is good to have good food again."

Evette was the only one to comment, "I'm sure it is, let me put another scoop on there."

Unlike me, it seemed the ladies had forgotten all the mean spirited things I'd said to many of them throughout the years. Lynelle was right, often the hardest part about forgiveness is forgiving yourself. I wondered if they had all been patiently waiting for the old Shay, the one who was kind and gentle and oh so sweet, to resurface, but I've got news for them, I plan to show them that an even more improved Shay was now onboard.

I believe I shocked everyone when I first boarded the bus with an overall, "Good Morning Ladies."

I'm sure they thought this was a result of my excitement of being free again, and figured it would wear off soon, but I'll prove them wrong if that's what they're thinking.

Sometimes you've got to set the atmosphere. Sometimes people feed off of your attitude, and your initial greeting. Some folks can be just as nasty if you're nasty to them, and then there are those who won't ever let you take them out of their kind spirit, they'll kill you with kindness every time.

Okay, I hear you Gramby.

It felt good to be included in the group, and truth be told I was the only one who had ever excluded myself, making myself the outcast.

Like everyone else I nodded and bobbed to all the different songs playing. When Evette put on the Impressions' "Keep On Pushing," everyone sang and some danced in the aisle of the bus.

Evette got right up in my face singing some parts of the song, causing me to laugh with her animation. *I've got to keep on pushing. I can't stop now. Move up a little higher, someway, somehow.*

Everyone belted out *Hallelujah, Hallelujah, keep on pushing!!*

The bus felt like it was rocking, and I couldn't remember the last time I laughed so hard. I still had some growing and changing to do. I still noticed things I noticed before, but learned not to comment on everything, and insult people. I still wondered where someone found a onesie that big, and I still wondered why at our age some folks wore their hair certain styles and colors, and I still couldn't get with the green and blue lipsticks at our age, but I learned to remember what Shay always said, it's all the similarities, and *differences* that brings out the beauty in all of us. I'm not like the next person, and she's not like me, but we're all wonderfully made.

Upon turning into the resort I saw an ambience that oozed of peace, something I hadn't had in my life for a long, long time. Of course, that was all due to my own self-inflicted actions. I heard the ladies talk about what we would be doing once we checked in and all that, but for a quick second I thought that I would be totally fine left outside to take in the waterfalls, flowers and greenery that left me saying, "Wow."

Brooklyn told me to hurry up because we had to be downstairs within the next fifteen minutes. I wanted to freshen up my hair and makeup, but she said, "Girl, we don't have time for all that, you look fine."

We were stepping fast through the hallways trying to get where we were going, of course, just as the evening when no one would tell Brooklyn where she was going for her birthday, I hadn't a clue where I was going either. I saw a sign that read, "Peaceful Waters." I didn't think much of the sign because all that I'd see of this resort so far was peaceful enough for me. Brooklyn motioned for me to turn this way and that way, until finally

I saw a few ladies from Girls in My Circle inside of a spa, there I'd find a larger sign, "Peaceful Waters."

"Brooklyn, I don't have money for this."

"Did anyone ask you anything about money?"

The young lady behind the counter asked Brooklyn if she had a reservation. "Yes, you should have reservations for both Brooklyn and Shay."

"Yes ma'am, I see you both on the list right here, please follow Tamora this way for your services."

In my excitement I said, "Brooklyn are you serious? Are you sure? I can wait to go to the spa when I can afford it."

"Yes Shay, I'm sure."

"But, you don't have to do this Brooklyn. I can do something else, or hang with some of the other ladies until you finish at the spa."

Brooklyn turned to me and said, "Are you still talking?"

We laughed.

Tamora extended her hand, "Ladies, there are lockers over here to put your items in. These robes and slippers are for you as well. You can take them with you after your service today. Please have a seat in the relaxation room out here when you're done changing, and help yourself to the fruit and beverages. Your name will be called shortly."

Almost giggling, I responded, "Thank you."

I tried to blink away the tears in my eyes; my emotions got the best of me. I couldn't imagine the kindness extended to me by others. I was in awe that folks still cared about my ol' crazy self after all the meanness I exuded for so long. Brooklyn noticed the tears and hugged me. Sometimes silence speaks louder than words. I don't know what she was thinking, or what words she would have said had she spoke, but I received it as her saying, "It's a new day Shay, let go of the past."

The manicure and pedicure were out of this world, but the deep tissue massage took me somewhere else. It felt so good. I heard a noise in the room, and stirred a bit on the table, only to find my snoring was the cause of the noise. Yes, it felt so good I zonked out. From that point I decided I would do whatever I could to stay awake, because I didn't want to sleep through this experience. I wanted to remember every single second of it all.

I couldn't stop thanking Brooklyn, "Thank you for inviting me Cousin. Thank you for loving me Cousin. Thank you for the spa treatment."

She finally told me, "Girl, you've already thanked me a hundred times, and we haven't even started the women's conference yet. You're going to really enjoy it."

I felt a sister type of love I hadn't felt in a long time, and I was glad to have dropped off some of the baggage I'd been lugging around for so many years to be able to enjoy this moment. After the spa treatment we were escorted to a beautiful banquet room where the banner said, "Happy Birthday Shay!"

I looked puzzled because it wasn't my birthday. My birthday was two months away. It reminded me of how mad Brooklyn got at me for the times I'd tell restaurant staff that it was her birthday, and it wasn't. They'd come with cake or ice cream with a candle on it singing, "Happy Birthday Dear Brooklyn, Happy Birthday to you!"

Brooklyn laughed at me. I'm sure the look on my face was that of pure confusion, "We know it's not your birthday, but we missed a few birthdays and thought this would be a good time to celebrate your 50th while we're all together."

I teared up, and tried to do a little speech.

"Thank you ladies, I just wanted to take a second to apologize…"

Evette cut me off, and said, "Forgive yourself. We forgave you a long time ago, just remember, the best apology is changed behavior."

I froze a bit thinking I've heard those words before. Of course Lynelle came to mind. She was definitely a friend worth having, and in six months she'd be inhaling freedom, too.

The women's conference was very nice. A lot of the speeches were geared towards women empowering one another. I recall one speaker saying, "When you see one of your fellow sisters fall, extend your hand to help her up, and if she's way down in the gutter, then shoot, give her both of your hands to help her up."

I felt the speaker was speaking directly to me. No doubt, Girls in My Circle had helped me up.

As we all exited the bus I was glad no police were waiting for me this time. I turned to the ladies and said "This was fun, when are we getting together again?"

"We've decided we don't need a reason to get together, we're going to do it more often *just because,* without a casket propped up in front of us, and without us saying, "We need to quit meeting like this. We can meet to bowl, line dancing, eat…anything. We're going to be like Nike and *Just Do It.*"

"Sounds Good."

I got off work, but had one more stop before making my way to the post office. Yes, work. Evette hired me at her group home. It's a very positive environment where we help women get back on their feet and prepare for the work force again. I assisted with helping them complete their applications, and resumes', but the part I liked the most was assisting them in putting on their make-up and doing their hair before the interviews. It was rewarding to help someone else feel good about them self. And, it was amazing that someone trusted me enough to hire me the way Evette did. I'm grateful.

Evette always had the same answer each time I, or anyone else, thanked her for giving us another chance, "Who am I not to give someone a chance, with all the chances people have given me. There's a reason I'm in this field, I was once one of these women."

One day a young lady at the facility named Sandy told me, "Thank you for helping us with our makeup and hair, you're beautiful."

I paused with emotion, and responded, "Yeah, but I have some stuff I've been working on on the inside that makeup can't cover up, so we're helping each other here. You're beautiful, too."

She gave me the sweetest hug that made me not want to let go. It felt sincere; it oozed of love and appreciation. Honestly there were times it made a tear roll down my face.

I made my way to Mother Griffin's porch and did that certain tap on the screen door we kids used to always do, "It's open baby, come on in."

She saw me through the screen door, yet didn't treat me any differently than she would anyone else, though to me she had good reason to. I apologized to her, and she accepted my apology. "Baby if the good Lord can forgive you and you can forgive yourself, then I surely can. I was wondering when you'd lose that ornery heifer you'd been dragging around with you. I'm just glad you lost her before I left this earth so I can see it with my own two eyes. You know the best apology is changed behavior."

"Yes ma'am."

I smiled, she hugged me, and said, "It's gonna be alright."

I'd have to agree with Brooklyn on that one, no one can say, "It's gonna be alright," like our mothers and Mrs. Griffin.

She continued, "You know life is simple, we're the ones who complicate things."

"Yes ma'am."

She rested her hand on top of mine, and I remembered all the days those hands combed my hair, got the sleep out of my eyes, or wiped the tears off my face. I also remembered all the days those hands popped me on my butt in correction.

This would be the beginning of a renewed relationship with Mrs. Griffin. As I stepped up my service to others I found myself at her house cleaning and doing things that I didn't want my own mother doing at her age.

Upon walking into the post office words I'd said too many times to count came to mind, "I don't do women." Yet, like Brooklyn said, "Go through something and see who's there for you. IT'S WHAT WOMEN DO!"

I pursed my lips and took a deep breath, thinking from whence I'd come, and excited about where I was going, no longer standing by that RED DOT trying to figure it out.

With thoughts whirling through my mind, I patiently pressed the label down on the large box full of items that people once took the time to send me.

I addressed it to the ladies in Pod 3984A. I proudly stuck the label on the left corner of the box.

From: GIRLS IN MY CIRCLE

The End

A friend is like a good bra:
Hard to find
Supportive
Comfortable
Always lifts you up
Makes you look better
Always close to your heart.

Girls In My Circle

When I was little,
I used to believe in the concept of one best friend.
And then I started to become a woman
And then I found out that if you allow your heart to open up,
God would show you the best in many friends.

She's The One

She's the one who will cry in a second for the happy things, and the sad.
She's the one who doesn't ever seem to crack.
She's the loudest in the group.
She's the quietest.
She's the one who dances as though no one is watching, regardless to what's going on.
She's the one who panics over everything.
She's the one who has all the barbecues.
She's looking for the barbecues.
She's the one who tries to pack all the leftovers away from the barbecues.
She's the sharp shooter.
She's the one who will sugarcoat things a bit to soften the blow.
She's the one who says whatever she wants.
She's the one you'll never know what's going on with her til' you ask.
She's the one who tells you everything about her, "I don't have anything to hide."
She's the one who wants to know everyone else's business, but never shares her own.
She's the one who laughs with you.
She's the one who laughs at you.
She's the one who is always in financial woes.
She's the one who can squeeze a dollar til' the president on it screams.
She's the one who shouts louder than you when you succeed.
She's the one always giving compliments.
She's the one who gets bashful when given a compliment.
She's the jokester.
She's the one who will not rest til' she gets the jokester back.
She's the one who will wipe the tears from your eyes.
She's the one who can't contain her tears and cries with you.
She's the one who gives the best advice in the world.
She's the one who doesn't take her own good advice.
She's the one who never seems to get upset.

She's the one who for some reason is upset about something all the time.

She's the one to come to the house when you've been down too long and tell you to get your butt up.

She's the one who is lady like, with a little bit of ghetto.

She's straight ghetto.

She's the one who will join you at the park or beach for a six mile walk.

She's the one who won't walk, but will join you for lunch after the walk.

She's the one who won't tell you your hair looks crazy, not to hurt your feelings.

She's the one who asks, "What's wrong with your hair?!!!"

She's the first to come see you in the hospital.

She's the one who will curl up all night in a chair in your hospital room.

She's the one who *just can't do hospitals*.

She's the one who struggles with her own self-esteem, but builds others up.

She's the one who always reels everyone back in and tells us to be the bigger person.

She's the one to say, "I'm tired of being the bigger person."

She's the one who slips you money privately.

She's the one who wants everyone to see what she's giving, not realizing that's for her own self glory.

She's the one who you can tell anything to.

She's the one who can't hold anything, so you've learned exactly what to trust her with.

She hates taking pictures.

She's always in front of a camera, posting every movement on Facebook.

She's always ready to duke it out to protect you, "Where they at?"

She's the one who has learned to pick her battles, and gently tells you "It's not worth it."

She's the one you talk to daily.

She's the one you might not talk to for weeks, months, years, but when you do things are the same.

She's the one who won't call you when you're mad. "She can stay mad!"

She's the one who will call you to tell you to stop the nonsense, iron things out and remind you tomorrow isn't promised.

She's that stranger in the restaurant, store, spa, park, who out of nowhere says something you needed to hear at that exact moment.

She's that little lady at church nearly twice your age that you pick on all the time, and everyone thinks is such an unlikely bond.
She will text.
She will email.
She will call.
But, she'll show up at your door.

She's family; she's from elementary school, junior high school, high school, college, church. She's a co-worker, the grocery store clerk; she's from the gym, the park, the beach, the doctor's office, or even the mall. She's someone you happened to meet through another friend, now you're the best of friends. She's my mother, my sister, my aunt, my friend, my cousin, my niece.

SHE'S ALL THE BEAUTIFUL LADIES who
make up the GIRLS IN MY CIRCLE.

By: Tracy Brooks

In Memory
Of
Ms. Cheryl Nelson
Dorsey High School, Los Angeles, CA - Class of 1980

There you were on your death bed still giving me scriptures to read.
"Read this every single day, and it will get you through some things. I'm
not kidding, I read it every single day, and I want you to do the same."
The last scripture you left me with:
Proverbs 4:20-23
Pay attention to what I say; turn your ear to my words. Do not let
them out of your sight; keep them within your heart; for they are
life to those who find them and health to one's whole body. Above
all else, guard your heart, for everything you do flows from it.

I'll cherish the memories my sister-friend.
I Hope You Dance!

As you plan your Girls in My Circle events, please send me a picture. I'd love to see them. TRACYS_DANCINGINTHERAIN@YAHOO.COM

CPSIA information can be obtained
at www.ICGtesting.com
Printed in the USA
BVHW070911160419
545655BV00001B/169/P

9 781532 064913